Tales from Eagle River

short stories

✳ ✳ ✳

by Melanie Lageschulte

Tales from Eagle River: short stories
© 2025
by Melanie Lageschulte
Fremont Creek Press

All rights reserved.

Kindle: 978-1-952066-40-5
Paperback: 978-1-952066-41-2
Hardcover: 978-1-952066-42-9
Large print paperback: 978-1-952066-43-6

Get notifications about new releases and more!
Sign up at fremontcreekpress.com/connect

Tales
from Eagle River

short stories

Also by Melanie Lageschulte

MAILBOX MYSTERIES SERIES
The Route That Takes You Home
The Road to Golden Days
The Lane That Leads to Christmas
The Path That Turns Toward Spring
Tales from Eagle River (*short stories*)

GROWING SEASON SERIES
Growing Season
Harvest Season
The Peaceful Season
Waiting Season
Songbird Season
The Bright Season
Turning Season
The Blessed Season
Daffodil Season
Firefly Season
A Tin Train Christmas (*short story*)

We Will Cross Here

✳ 1858 ✳

Her head was spinning long before the ferry reached the far shore. Torrential rains had fallen two days ago, and the Eagle River was still high on its banks and its current was relentlessly swift. The ferry platform bobbed like a cork as Lena's husband and his friend speared their long poles into the muddy river bottom, pushed forward as far as they could, then tried again.

Lena Baxter wasn't the only one who was afraid. The horses' dark eyes were wide and wild as the agitated water attacked the bottom of the ferry, which wasn't much more than a series of wooden planks lashed together. Even Adam's gentle words to the team couldn't silence their anxious neighs.

Somewhere in the middle of the river, Lena realized she had to let go. Not of the wagon's wooden bench, not until she felt the earth back under its wheels.

But her fear? It was of no use to her out here.

They'd been traveling for almost a week, by stagecoach and now wagon. The July days had been relentlessly humid, and the mosquitoes had been vicious last night despite the heavy smoke from the travelers' campfire. Lena was sweaty and dirty, and exhausted. But she hadn't made it all this way across the Iowa prairie only to topple headfirst off a raft and drown in these raging, algae-infested waters only yards from her destination.

Land, at last. While Clem Bradford soothed the horses, Adam reached for his wife's hand and guided her toward the wagon's metal step.

He gave her a wide smile, and she wondered how much of it came from relief. But then, she remembered her husband had been piloting ferry boats for a decade already, since he was fifteen. Those savings from his humble beginnings in Ohio had been greatly multiplied through investments in stagecoach lines, and now the railroad.

Adolphus Baxter was a well-respected businessman, even at such a young age. This latest venture, which included founding a town on the banks of the Eagle River and securing a stop on a future railroad line, would be one more feather in his cap.

Money and opportunity brought choices. And Lena's husband had decided several years ago that he wasn't overly fond of his first name. He'd remade his image, fattened his bank accounts; if he wanted to twist Adolphus into something simpler, more refined, who would dare to stop him?

"Be careful, my love." Adam placed a gentle hand on Lena's elbow as she navigated the wagon's narrow step. "You'll need a moment to get your land legs back after that."

The heel of her once-polished boot, which had been caked in dirt for days, narrowly missed becoming trapped in a hole in the soft vegetation along the wagon road. Well, it wasn't much of a road; more like a set of wheel tracks that looked as if they would be easily erased by the prairie grass within a few days of not being used.

Lena quickly regained her balance, then pointed into the weeds.

"A prairie dogs' burrow, I'd guess. It's the right size. See that other hole, five feet to the right? That's another entrance to their tunnels."

Clem gave Adam a good-natured punch on the arm as he wandered past to check the wagon's cargo hadn't shifted during the crossing. "Caught yourself a bright one, eh, Adam? She'll be tracking deer and pheasants before you know it."

Clem's observation had been paired with an easy laugh, but Lena caught an undercurrent of something in his voice. Scorn, perhaps. Jealousy? Most definitely.

Clem had never had the benefit of formal schooling, and could only sign documents with an "X." That included the certificate for the Baxters' wedding. The judge had notarized Clem's mark, of course; and Lena's sister, Anna, had added her signature with a flourish.

Adam and Lena had been husband and wife for three weeks now, but Lena sometimes got the feeling they weren't properly married, after all. And sometimes, as she lay next to him in the middle of the night, wide awake, she pondered the leap of faith she'd taken to tie herself to this man.

Lena missed Anna already. It seemed like forever ago that they'd attended Miss Easton's finishing school, and spent their afternoons sipping tea with their friends and waltzing the nights away at balls attended by the Dubuque's elite. How Adam had managed to get an invitation to Lady Wilson's winter solstice dance, Lena still wasn't sure.

His admittance had been due to "a friend's generosity," Adam merely said whenever anyone asked how he and Lena had met. For all Lena knew, Adam had snuck in through the servants' quarters in evening dress he'd won off somebody in a card game. He'd swept Lena off her feet; first during a run of the Virginia Reel, and later on the terrace when no one else was around.

Adam had moved away to give instructions to the men who would unload the wagon at the Baxters' cabin, and Lena was grateful to have a few moments to herself. Sweat trickled through her hastily secured honey-blond hair and down her neck; her wide-brimmed straw hat blocked the sun, but not the sweltering air. She envied the men, in their loose shirts and pants, and tried to adjust her corset to keep the stays from digging further into her skin.

Tired of the heat, Lena had ditched her traveling gloves two days ago. Her mother would have been horrified.

She glanced down at her palms, which were dry and dirty, and prepared herself for how chapped and rough they were going to become. This new life was going to be filled with hard work; her hands would never be the same.

Lena was eager to see the cabin, which Adam had built in the spring, then decided she could wait a few minutes more. Several, in fact. Because whatever she found inside was going to be her new home and, despite her husband's assurances that the abode was the very best one in the settlement, it was going to be nowhere near as comfortable as her parents' grand townhouse.

Instead, she studied the clearing in front of her and the men hard at work within it.

Just west of here, the forest gave way to the wide prairies; but the early settlers continued to clear the land in this location so the town would sit within easy walking distance of the river. Four men across the way were chopping down trees this afternoon. Another team, made up of those who looked to still be in their teens, were digging out stumps. Certain trees had been spared, at least, providing some shade for the rough-hewn cabins and canvas-flapped tents scattered around the clearing.

She had a touch of the imagination, as Mother had always said with a downturn of the mouth that hinted such a skill wasn't required of a lady; but Lena suspected this piece of land wouldn't easily transform itself into an outpost of civilization.

Adam had returned, and his tanned face was so alight with excitement that Lena bit back her potential commentary regarding the mosquitoes, and the heat, and the unavoidable stench coming from the log-walled shack nearby that served as a barn for the little village's prized livestock.

"We'll go home in a little while," he promised. "But first, I have something very important to show you."

He waved Clem over, and the three of them set off toward the east and south, back to the river, following a ragged footpath into the woods. Lena soon heard the river murmuring to itself, then a rushing sound, and then the sharp slaps of the water as it battled the rock-studded shoreline while making its way south.

Lena had only ever lived in St. Louis and Dubuque. In both cities, the Mississippi River was the engine that drove their economies. But that wide waterway had been so far from her family's homes that one could almost forget it was there. But here, she realized now, the Eagle River would always be at the forefront of her life. And its whims might determine if this little village would thrive, or vanish from the map.

The woods soon opened to reveal a narrow shoreline of sunbaked earth crisscrossed with animal tracks. If she took off her boots and tiptoed ahead a few more feet, Lena could have felt the cool slime of the riverbed's edge under her toes. There was a distinctive smell in the air, of hot sunshine and algae and mud.

Despite the brackish odor, the river bottoms teemed with life and activity. Even here, right along the edge, small fish darted through the rippling water. A weathered turtle that looked as if it had been born in prehistoric times sunned itself on a small boulder a few feet away. Dragonflies' iridescent wings glinted in the afternoon light as they hovered over the river's surface. A cacophony arose from the trees as several species of birds gossiped about the three strangers who had appeared in their midst.

If only she could fly, Lena thought as she surveyed the churning water. The precarious ferry ride rushed through her mind, and she took a quick step back from the shore.

Adam, who had amazed Lena many times with his seemingly clairvoyant ability to read her emotions, put an arm around his wife.

"The river isn't always this volatile. The water's high right now; but sometimes, it's as smooth as a pond, and less deep. I know our crossing was rather ... exciting," he said with a wry grin that made Lena give a small laugh and shake her head, "but we are going to fix that."

"In more ways than one," Clem pronounced with a sudden air of confidence as he and Adam exchanged a triumphant glance. "A real bridge isn't even the half of it."

Adam guided Lena a few feet to the right, then gently nudged her to stop.

"Now, look across the river, right here. What do you see?"

"Trees? Mud? Oh, there's another bird, right there in that oak." She pointed it out to the men, another casual gesture that would have caused Mother to reach for her smelling salts. "It's some sort of jay, I believe."

"Someday, hopefully very soon, you're going to see much more than that." Adam took a dramatic pause. "Lena, my dear, the railroad is definitely coming to Eagle River. The negotiations are done, all the papers have been signed."

"We will cross here." Clem rubbed his hands together in anticipation. "It's the perfect place for the trestle. The ferry crossing is at the narrowest part of the channel, but those banks are a bit steeper than these."

"Those are fine for wagons and horses," Adam explained, "but not an iron horse."

He let out a whoop of joy. "But this is perfect! The approach, on both sides, is nearly flat. That means less earthwork needed to ensure the tracks are level. The line will come northwest from Cedar Falls, and it's going to be built right through our little town."

"Eagle River won't be little for long," Clem predicted. "Think of it: The tracks cross the river here, then come into town on the south side. The depot will be along Second Street."

"The depot?" Lena couldn't help but catch the men's excitement. "Like a lean-to, or ..."

"Way more than that," Clem promised. "A real frame building, with windows all along the front, and a sheltered porch that comes right out to the tracks. I think we should have a separate waiting room for the ladies."

"Frank gets to decide," Adam reminded Clem. The Sonbergs were another of the town's founding families and also investors in the railroad. "He's going to manage the depot, after all."

Railroads were the way of the future, Lena knew. Just last year, a line had crossed the Mississippi River and reached Dubuque. It would be a few years before any tracks came as far as Eagle River, but that access would make everything easier for this burgeoning town. Faster delivery of crops to market, and supplies coming back the other way. And for Lena, a far more pleasant journey home.

But this is my home now, she reminded herself. *Here, with Adam. I made my choice, and I will see this through.*

On a bright summer's day like this one, it was an easy vow to make. Lena quickly pushed the opposing side of that thought to the back of her mind. And while the river would certainly always be a vital part of this village, Lena realized, it was the railroad that would enable, or crush, its very existence.

"Is everything truly in order?" The hint of caution in Clem's voice caught Lena's attention. "I know a few of the other investors still had some questions."

"It's all been handled." Adam waved away his friend's concerns. "I took care of that, back in Dubuque. Everyone has been mollified. Some little advances on our future profits went a long way in that regard. I made a special trip to the land office, too."

"Is there anything I need to do?" Clem was eager to spring into action. "If I need to head back there, have a few conversations ..."

Adam laughed. "You can stand down. We're not going to have any problems. Not like before."

A shiver ran down Lena's spine despite the heat.

What exactly had her husband and his associates done, or promised, to ensure the railroad came through this town? Eagle River was so new, so unformed, that it had yet to appear on any map.

It was all a mystery to Lena, and that bothered her.

She read the newspapers; she knew railroads were far more than the promise of the future. They cost big money, and big favors. And she'd spent enough time eavesdropping outside Father's office to know men often took dangerous gambles to secure significant paydays.

Lena had yet to meet Frank, although that was going to happen this afternoon. Frank, who was from Illinois, was a whiz with numbers and budgets, Adam had told Lena, and it was to his credit that the trio's transportation investments had done so well these past several years.

Clem was quite the puzzle: Whip-smart despite his lack of schooling, with an efficient way of managing situations that bordered on ruthlessness. Clem was one of Adam's childhood friends, and had apparently been quite the bare-knuckle boxing champ until he'd grown tired of having his nose reset.

Given the sudden, ominous swerve in Adam and Clem's conversation, Lena wondered if they had forgotten she was within earshot. But she turned back from the water's edge to see them both staring at her with expectant looks on their faces.

"What do you think?" Adam wanted to know. "Can you see it? What Eagle River is going to become?"

Lena had made her own gamble, and it was time to double down.

"Yes. Yes, I can." She grasped his hand, and saw his shoulders relax. "This little village is going to be at the crossroads of this entire region one day. And we can say we were here to see it happen."

"To *make* it happen," Adam said with a grin while Clem nodded his approval of Lena's brief speech.

"You know," Clem offered, "there's still time to change the town plat. Eagle River's fine, of course. the obvious choice. But 'Baxter's Landing' has a certain charm, as well."

"Oh, there's no need for that." The humility in Adam's response seemed genuine. "I can make my mark here without taking things that far." He shrugged. "Besides, 'landing' has the feel of a ferry to it, you know? Boat travel of some kind. And the railroad is the future."

"How about Baxter Junction, then?" Lena suggested with a playful elbow jab to her husband's side.

Adam brushed that off as well, but Clem considered it. "Well, we might have to have two rail lines for that. Maybe that's pushing things a little too far."

"At least for now," Adam said.

"Then I vote for it to stay Eagle River," Lena proclaimed as they walked back to the center of the village. "And I'm eager to get a look at the majestic birds' nests. I've read they are quite the feat of engineering."

The waterway had been named several years ago by the fur trappers who were the first white men in the area. While the eagles were comfortably at home all along the river, they tended to congregate close to the site of the future mill. The small rapids there offered the birds prime fishing grounds.

Clem was soon called away by one of the men felling trees, and Adam and Lena followed another walking path toward a cabin on the south edge of the clearing. And there, Lena spotted a welcome sight: A woman was hanging her washing on a rope tied between two trees. Two girls played in the dirt around her feet, and the woman was clearly carrying another child. Despite the weariness in her eyes, she returned Lena's relieved smile.

"That's Carrie Sonberg," Adam told Lena. "Caroline, actually; but we don't stand on ceremony out here. She's a little older than you, but I think the two of you are going to be good friends."

Lena momentarily wondered why men always assumed women were close friends just because of their proximity to each other. But here, in this remote and wild place, she decided Adam was right. She and Carrie were the only women in the camp, at least for the foreseeable future.

"And there's Frank." Adam waved at a man a decade older who was patching the wood shakes on his cabin's roof. Frank backed down his wood-pole ladder and motioned for his two boys to join him. As he reached the footpath, Frank pulled a pair of spectacles from his shirt pocket.

"Ma'am." He greeted Lena with a firm handshake and a shy smile. "It's good to finally meet you. Carrie's been asking after you, as well."

"I'll be sure to stop by tomorrow," Lena promised. "Once I get settled."

Frank's sudden, sharp laugh rang through the clearing. "Forgive me for saying so, but I'm afraid you aren't going to be 'settled' for quite some time. Maybe it won't take long to unpack, but life out here is bound to keep you on your toes."

The boys, both in their mid-teens, had caught up to their father. "This is George and Henry," Frank said proudly. "The best construction assistants a man could hope for."

"I think you'll find Eagle River a thrilling place to live," George told Lena as he boldly stepped forward to shake her hand. "Between all the wild animals lurking about, and the Indians ..."

Adam sighed. "Thanks for scaring my wife." He turned to Lena. "Don't worry, they've moved on."

"Mostly," George corrected him.

"Mostly," Adam repeated. "They've been relocated, as you know. A few turn up from time to time. But we haven't had any trouble here. We stick to our business, and they stick to theirs."

"And the creatures?" Lena addressed her question to George, who seemed eager to remain part of the adults' conversation. "What's lurking around out here in the dark?"

"Oh, you know." George looked around, as if expecting something to emerge from the woods at that very moment. "Foxes, raccoons. The badgers are the worst, ma'am. They're nasty if they get cornered."

Lena reconsidered her evaluation of the hole she'd nearly stepped in as she'd dismounted the wagon. A chattering little prairie dog would be most welcome by comparison.

"The jack rabbits do make for good eating," Frank mused, then moved slightly closer to Lena and away from his boys.

"The others, well ... we had more trouble with them last winter; not as much since the spring thaw. But it's better to not roam about at night."

"There are panthers around," Henry suddenly said, and Lena saw the fear in the boy's eyes. "The black ones aren't so common; it's mostly the tan ones." He pointed to where another footpath exited the woods. "Jackson found a strange pile of scat one morning, not long ago. Said it was too big to be from the wolves, and too small to be from a bear."

"Jacob Kempel's boy is quite the storyteller," Frank told Lena with a side glance at Adam. "He certainly can spin a yarn."

But Henry's face told Lena the truth.

"Thank you, Henry, for the warning." She gave the boy a wide smile, and got a small one in return. "I'll be sure to keep inside by the fire once the sun goes down. And I'd love to learn more about the wildlife in the area. Maybe you can help me with that."

"How about we see the town, first?" Adam seemed eager

to change the subject. "Most of the stakes have been set out."

Lena wrapped her hand through the crook of his elbow. The weave of Adam's homespun shirt was coarse under her arm. "I'd be delighted, sir. Let's start back at the road."

* * *

They took another trail through the rough grass to reach the east-west wagon track that had brought them from the ferry and into the village. Lena had been too distracted before, but she now noticed the foot-high, rough-hewn wooden sticks that dotted the clearing at set intervals.

"This is First Street." Adam put one boot down in the mud of the tracks, carefully avoiding a startled bumblebee that had been dining on a clump of nearby clover. "It stretches from the river landing to the west edge of the clearing. And someday, it will go far beyond that."

They turned west, and soon arrived at another set of sticks. "And this," Adam paused for dramatic effect, "is Main Street."

The town's future thoroughfare wasn't much more than another set of wagon tracks that went north to meet the river. The Kempels' mill was under construction along the south bank; eventually, a bridge would cross the river somewhere near the mill.

"Jacob and Matthew hope to have the main structure closed in, and the water wheel in place, before winter," Adam told his wife. The humid breeze carried the slaps of the hammers and the shouts of the men.

"They will process wheat, eventually, for flour. We'll use it to create our own lumber, too. Log cabins are fine to start, but this town is going to have real buildings. In more ways than one."

Lena looked around the clearing. "Where is the kiln? You'd mentioned bricks ..."

"The Kleiner brothers have found the perfect spot for

their business. It's just south of town, along the river. They hope to be fully operational sometime next year. That's the end goal: a town filled with brick buildings. They're warmer in the winter, and better able to stand up to the wind, too."

"I've noticed how strong it is out here." Lena checked that the ties on her wide-brimmed hat were still securely fastened under her chin. "I would think brick buildings greatly reduce the risk of fire, as well."

"Exactly."

As they strolled south, Adam shared his vision for the little town.

Thomas Starling carried a small selection of dry goods in the front room of his cabin, and he was hard at work on an addition that would be the town's first store. Work on a real mercantile would start as soon as the kiln had produced enough bricks.

They'd received word that a blacksmith, a cousin of one of the current men in the town, was moving to Eagle River in the spring. The depot would be built over there, a few blocks off Main Street. And this corner would be the perfect spot for a school ...

A flock of chickens, fat from the plentiful insects and lush grass, clucked and flapped their way across the couple's path. Josie, the community cow, gave a greeting from the patch of shade where she grazed with her calf. An indignant squirrel in an oak tree supervised with sharp eyes while a group of men planed logs by hand for another building.

Adam and Lena soon approached a snug cabin just down the path from the Sonbergs' home. "Mrs. Baxter," he said proudly, "we've arrived at the final stop on our tour."

Although the cabin was flanked by several proud oak trees, Lena could still see the glint of the bright sun off its two compact windows. She blinked away a few happy tears when she spotted a scrap of a rose bush by the front door.

Her grandmother had brought cuttings of a fuchsia-bloomed shrub from Germany some twenty years ago. Lena had had her doubts when Adam promised to transfer a delicate shoot from her parents' formal garden to this wild place that was to be her new home. But as with most things her new husband attempted, he'd followed through on his promise.

There were no blooms on the small shrub, not yet; and there might not be any this year. But its stem was straight and proud, and the branches wreathed with healthy leaves told Lena the plant's roots were already established in this foreign soil.

Lena steeled herself for a different sort of surprise as they entered the cabin. She knew it would be primitive, but that may not be the worst of it. Adam had been living a bachelor's life inside these walls, and Lena feared finding a mess of dirty dishes and boot-tracked clods of mud on the planed-log floors.

She was relieved when she passed through the doorway and saw just the opposite.

The main room was backed by a stunning stone fireplace and hearth that Adam had built from rocks turned up along the river's banks. The pots and pans looked as if they'd been scrubbed spotless with sand. Everything was neatly arranged on the hooks and shelves.

Two rocking chairs waited by the fireplace, and Lena's two trunks now sat at attention in the corner by the table. In the tiny second room, the bed quilt was clean and smooth.

"It's wonderful." Lena was somewhat surprised to realize she meant it. As humble as this cabin was, she truly could see herself living here. "You must have been up all hours of the night, getting it ready, before you came to fetch me."

While Adam had been playing tour guide since they'd arrived in Eagle River, his time was normally spent out with the other men, felling trees, chopping wood, tending to the animals.

"Well, you know I like things to be orderly. And I had a little help," Adam admitted with a sheepish grin. "I asked Carrie for her unvarnished opinion, several times over. She had no qualms about telling me what's what."

"I like her already."

Adam gestured for Lena to take one of the two chairs pushed under the square table, and brought them both tin cups of water. It was cold and clear, with a distinctive sweetness that made Lena's eyebrows dart up in surprise.

"It's spring water. There's quite the aquifer running under this town, we discovered. All three of the wells we've dug have easily tapped it. We have everything here that we could ever need."

Lena looked around at their humble cabin. So much of what she was accustomed to was missing. Even so, Adam was right. And, she realized, there was something new here, something that she never could have obtained back in her old life: freedom.

She wasn't going to spend her days organizing afternoon teas, and agonizing over place cards for a sit-down dinner for forty almost-strangers. The tradeoff, however, was that there wouldn't be maids, or wet nurses for the babies that were sure to come, or family close by to lend emotional support and several extra pairs of hands.

But there was already a strong sense of community in this little village, one that was sure to grow as more people settled here.

Lena was going to have to rely on herself now, more than she ever had before. And on this man who sat across from her. This handsome, intelligent, charming man that she knew just well enough to marry, but not yet well enough to see exactly how they would complement each other through all the decades of life to come.

He was waiting for her to say something, she could sense that. All day, Adam had been looking to Lena for approval, for assurance that she believed in his dream and shared it with him. That she was ready for this challenge.

"You're right." She covered his hand with one of her own. "We do have everything we need. Especially because we have each other."

"That we do."

And then his smile faltered, just a bit. "Well, there is ... something else."

"Oh, my!" Lena widened her eyes dramatically. "It's been a day full of surprises. What is it?"

Adam went to a nearby shelf and reached for a slim leather portfolio. He pulled out a piece of heavy, cream-colored paper, carefully unfolded it, and placed it on the table.

"I have a proposition for you, my love. You've already taken me up on the most important proposal, the one where you said you'd be my wife. Coming out here with me runs a close second. But this decision, I hope, will be a much easier one for you to make."

Lena leaned over to study the paper. It was an application, one that had already been signed by her husband's angular handwriting.

"A post office?" She sat back in her chair for a moment, took it all in. "You're saying that on top of helping manage the mercantile, and overseeing the coming of the railroad, that you want to be a postmaster, too? It's a wonderful idea," she added quickly. "A post office is a sign of civilization, one that will be needed in Eagle River. But how are you ever going to get it all done?"

Adam looked at the floor. "Well," he finally said, "I was hoping you, dear Lena, would agree to take that on."

Lena stared at her husband in shocked silence for several moments. "Me? But I'll have so much to do, here at home." She shook her head. "Besides, I'm not sure if women ..."

"That's my point, exactly. With my name on it, this

application is certain to be approved. This is too important to leave to chance, Lena. Other towns will start up in this area one day, especially along the rail line. Eagle River is going to need every advantage we can give it to make it thrive."

And then, Adam leaned in with a confident smile.

"You have given up so much to come here. I want you to have your own piece of it, beyond just our home; a way to make your own mark on this town." He chuckled. "And besides, I'd guess you're the most educated person here, even more so than Frank."

"Miss Easton's school prepared me to host balls and paint watercolors," Lena reminded her husband. "That bit of French I learned? I doubt it's going to come in handy out here on the prairie."

They both stared at the application for a moment. It was just a piece of paper, there in the middle of the table, but it held so much promise.

Finally, Adam shrugged. "This is how it is: We work within the systems that are in place, right? And work around them when they haven't yet caught up to what we want to do."

Lena was excited about this unexpected opportunity. But she couldn't help but notice that, despite Adam's complete confidence in her ability to handle this task, he hadn't talked to her before he filled out the application.

If they were truly partners, truly equals, shouldn't they have discussed this beforehand?

Lena had never given it a moment's thought before, but she couldn't be certain women were prohibited from serving as postmasters. What if the application offered up her name instead, and it somehow was approved?

But it was too late now. Adam's insistence that everything went according to his plans didn't leave room for the possibility of Lena being allowed to fully embrace this challenge on her own.

It irritated her, no doubt. But she was smart enough to

tamp down her aspirations. *No matter where you go,* she reminded herself, *some things never change.*

Lena had reinvented herself, upended her entire existence; but the outside world only saw that she'd moved from her father's house to her husband's house. As a woman, Lena wasn't anywhere as close to being in charge of her fate as she'd like to be.

"There are others that could step up to help," Adam said. "And there won't be much to do, not at first. Although someday, that's going to change."

Even as she questioned her husband's choices, Lena recognized the potential of what was being asked of her.

She could see herself behind a small counter in one corner of the mercantile, helping residents prepare letters to send home to their loved ones. The excitement everyone would feel on those days when a wagon arrived bearing letters gathered at the nearest larger town. And someday, full mailbags would arrive by train.

"It doesn't matter what it says on that sheet of paper," she said. "I'll do it. And to the best of my ability."

Adam suddenly got to his feet. She did the same.

"Mrs. Lena Baxter," he intoned in a solemn voice as they laughed and shook hands, "I hereby appoint you to serve as Eagle River's first postmaster."

"And I gladly accept."

The sun had dropped lower outside the cabin's windows. Beyond the still-open door, the birds were starting to sing their evening songs. Lena looked around her husband's broad shoulders to where the cast-iron cook stove waited along the wall.

"I'm proud to inform you that I make excellent pancakes," she told her husband.

"As for other things, well ... Here's what you can do for me, in return for me becoming this village's first postmaster: I'm going to need you to teach me how to cook."

Vigil

* 1861 *

It was the silence, pressing in all around her, that caused Helen to open her eyes. Outside the cabin, the October darkness was as still as the dead. There were no crickets marking one of the last nights before a hard frost arrived, and no calls from the owls posted in the trees along the river.

Inside the cabin, it was also strangely quiet. Pierre was barely snoring, for once; and certainly not the way he usually did after too much whiskey. Thankfully, he hadn't reached for the hem of Helen's nightgown after stumbling in from the revelry he'd enjoyed with old Mr. Schmidt and the Kempels' two grown sons.

No one else in this little village seemed to notice, or be concerned about, the raucous gatherings that often ran into the wee hours. But every swig of whiskey Pierre enjoyed reminded Helen that her marriage was a nightmare.

She slipped out of bed, and her bare feet searched the cabin's hard-packed earthen floor until they found her moccasins. The shoes were one of the few things from Helen's past life, her Lakota life far to the west, that she had managed to save.

After her father died, her mother took up with a white man. A cruel man who, two years ago when Helen was fifteen, traded her to fur trapper Pierre Boucher for what the

Frenchman claimed was the best team of oxen west of the Missouri River.

"Winona," Helen whispered as she buried her toes in the moccasins. It was her Lakota name, her true name, given to her by her grandmother, her *unci*. Calling herself by that name, even if no one else ever did again, reminded her who she really was.

Her real name meant "firstborn daughter," Unci had always said with pride. As a little girl, Winona had felt special, valued. Not anymore.

Pierre was the one who had decided Winona should become Helen. He'd dictated the change just before he marched her in front of the traveling priest who passed through the Lakota's land a few times a year. Suddenly, she was as French, and Catholic, as Pierre; and he had a piece of paper to prove it.

Pierre's occupation meant Helen was often left to fend for herself for several days at a time, and she had been grateful for that. But trapping had become increasingly difficult as more white men moved west. The Bouchers had roamed for a few months, ultimately crossing the Missouri River into western Iowa, where Pierre set up a more permanent camp on the land claim of a new settler.

Helen still wasn't sure if her husband had known the circumstances attached to the place where they'd pitched their tent; but when the old German man and his adult son showed up to take possession of their property, Pierre hadn't hesitated to shoot them both.

And so, while white people were moving west in search of a new life, Pierre and Helen had come a long way east looking for their own escape.

When they'd arrived in Eagle River five months ago, Pierre purchased a small plot on the west edge of the settlement that included a neglected, cramped cabin, the community's only uninhabited dwelling. Helen had never seen so many brick buildings in one place before she came to Eagle River, but it seemed appropriate that she and Pierre lived in the worst home the village offered. Because the Bouchers were never going to fit into this close-knit community.

Here, Pierre repeated the story that Helen was French, like himself. People had either been kind enough, or disinterested enough, to pretend they believed it; or they didn't see the Bouchers as worth even a moment of their scrutiny.

Helen's dark hair and eyes didn't exactly give her away, as she dressed and did her hair like a white woman. She spoke a great deal of French, which most people in Eagle River couldn't understand, and a small amount of the English they all knew so well. Her moccasins stayed in the cabin, always hidden under the bed when the rare visitor arrived at their door.

She checked that Pierre was still sound asleep, then padded to their cabin's lone window. The moon was full; the small yard that she took such care to keep tidy glowed with an unearthly light. The great oaks that towered over it had shed nearly all their leaves, and their bare branches swayed in the wind.

No one seemed to be about at this hour. No humans, anyway.

A shrill howl soon echoed through the nearby woods, and Helen knew the wolves were on the move tonight. While the white man's arrival in this river valley had pushed many of the larger wild animals farther out onto the prairie, the wolves hadn't been so quick to retreat. In their own way, they still held claim to the land in and around Eagle River.

Last winter had been terribly brutal, she'd heard, and the wolves had been especially tenacious. They'd boldly roamed the village's streets after dark in search of scraps; and more than one terrified resident had opened their back door just before dawn to find a wolf or two bunking behind their woodpile.

Helen knew the creatures could be vicious. They deserved a wary respect and a wide berth. Even so, their intelligence and hunting skills were to be admired. They held a place of honor in the Lakota world, as did most of the other creatures of the fields and skies.

Helen liked to believe the wolves that roamed these woods were determined to regain their rightful place in the order of things. If only the native human residents would be allowed to do the same. After all, this had been Winnebago land before they were pushed out and away.

Another mournful call echoed through the cracks in the cabin's walls. Then three more.

Pierre didn't even stir. Helen's husband didn't fear the wolves the way many of the white folks did, probably due to his time way out west where the animals were still so plentiful. In her darker moments, Helen hoped his careless attitude might someday be her salvation.

If only Pierre would wander out alone at night, drunk and disoriented, and startle the pack as they slipped through the woods ...

Two of the animals howled again, and Helen was now certain she knew where they were gathering tonight: a small clearing across the river, up on the ridge just north of the sawmill. It was one of the pack's favorite nocturnal locations. It was also a desolate, lonely place that lured Helen's only true friend away from home on restless nights like this one.

Helen traded her moccasins for her sturdy boots, checked that her folded knife was secure in the pocket of her nightgown, and lifted her wool coat from its peg before she slipped out the cabin door.

The fresh, cool air caught in her throat for a moment, but she welcomed it nonetheless. The cabin was warmer, of course; but it was thick with the lingering smell of Pierre's after-supper pipe and the rancid odor of his still-damp boots drying by the fireplace.

It only took a few moments for Helen's eyes to adjust to the darkness, and she soon let the light of the moon guide her to the main wagon path through town, then north toward the mill.

Some of the residents didn't feel safe on the wooden bridge that crossed the river by the rapids, especially when the wind was strong. The bridge had been hastily constructed, Helen had heard, to replace an even more precarious ferry crossing that had been on the east side of town. She listened to the swish-swish of the river as it splashed through the falls and under the bridge, but didn't dare look down.

There were just two cabins on the far side of the river, and then the woods quickly pressed in on the narrow road. Here, far away from the center of the village, the animals of the night were more active.

Helen sensed, rather than saw, the fox that tiptoed through the brush on the side of the path. The splash behind her was a beaver entering the water, and the dark shadow gliding over her was an owl on its nocturnal hunting rounds.

The knife in her pocket felt like an unnecessary weight against the creatures of the forest. Because Helen, in her own way, was one of them. She was more at peace here, in the dark woods, than walking Eagle River's muddy streets in the daylight.

The wolves called again, and Helen hurried her steps as she climbed the gradual rise that beckoned her toward the clearing. Ahead in the gloom, she spotted the fragile light of a small lantern, then a form bending low in front of a large rock.

As Helen drew near, Violet Hendricksen lifted one palm in greeting. Violet's other hand, Helen knew, had a firm grip on the hunting rifle cradled in her lap.

"I thought you might be here," Helen whispered as she

assumed her usual post at Violet's side. Violet only knew English, but that had given Helen a chance to improve her own vocabulary. "I heard the wolves."

In the dim glow of the lantern, Helen could see the deep shadows under Violet's eyes.

"I've been expecting them," Violet whispered as she pushed a few stray blond hairs under her knit cap. "It's been three nights since they gathered here last. I had to come." She was dressed in more layers than Helen, her slight form bundled against the hours of cold darkness she would endure before sunrise.

On the edge of the small clearing, two golden eyes reflected the lantern's feeble light. Then three more pairs. And a fifth set of eyes, more restless and higher off the ground. One of the pack's larger males was in attendance tonight.

As the girls stared at him, the alpha raised his snout and let out a hair-raising howl. Violet's skirts rustled as she gripped the gun with both hands.

"If he dares to come out here," she said in a low, cold voice, "I'll shoot him dead."

"You don't want to do that."

"I'm a good shot. I can take him down, if I must."

Violet was petite, she wasn't much more than a wisp of a girl at seventeen years of age, but Helen knew her friend was the crack shot she claimed to be.

How many times had they had this same conversation, here in this weed-choked clearing, over the past three months?

Helen couldn't remember, and didn't want to. Because then, she'd have to acknowledge that Violet, her only ally in this godforsaken wide spot in the road, was losing her grip on reality.

"You won't need to shoot him, or the others." As she put a hand on her friend's slight shoulder, Helen kept her tone gentle. Violet's nerves were always razor sharp on wild nights like this. "The wolves are just curious about us. They were here first, as you know, before all these people arrived. They mean us no harm."

"That's not true!" Violet's words broke off into a sob. "You know why they're here, and so do I. I'm not going to let them take my baby!"

The rock in front of them was the only sort of weatherproof tombstone that could be easily acquired in this remote place. Violet's husband had dug it out of the riverbed, then some of the other men helped him load it on a cart and bring it up the hill. Tears had streamed down Joseph's face as he'd whittled the stone with shaking hands: "Amelia - 1861."

There hadn't been any reason to add anything more. Nothing chiseled on a stone was going to change what had happened.

Helen had rushed to the Hendricksens' cabin that hot July afternoon when Violet's labor started; Mrs. Kempel, one of their closest neighbors, wasn't far behind. While Helen and Joseph tried to comfort Violet, Ingrid Kempel had stayed busy changing the soaked sheets, praying aloud for God's mercy upon her young neighbor, and urging Violet to push at the right times.

As the ordeal dragged on, it became clear something was terribly wrong. Violet was too small to easily deliver the child, and the closest doctor was a hard day's ride away. The baby finally arrived in a rush of blood, gave one mewling cry, then fell silent in Mrs. Kempel's arms.

"The wolves aren't going to take Amelia," Helen told Violet. "They can't get to her. She's too far down, remember? The men made sure of that."

Helen had watched Joseph and another man dig a hole into this hillside that was well over three feet deep, quite a feat for such a small opening in the ground. The hurriedly constructed pine box had been tiny, too.

Violet's fear that the wolves would steal her dead baby might seem outlandish, the hysterical ravings of a grief-stricken girl; but it held more than a hint of justifiable concern.

Helen remembered how, in hushed tones, the men had discussed that very possibility as they'd started to dig the grave. If it was too shallow, there would be the risk of a scent. At least, until ...

"That's what Joseph said." Violet's tone made it clear she wasn't ready to believe either her friend or her husband. "He says it has been too long now, that the time of worry is long past. But you know how cunning those monsters are."

And where was Joseph now? Probably at home, lying awake; distraught in his own way and unable to cope with the loss of his child or support his grief-stricken wife. Joseph was young, but Helen knew he was one of the good men in this town. She might be able to give poor Joseph a pass.

But some of the other villagers had to know about Violet's long nights on this hill with the wolves. Why hadn't something been done?

And then, Helen decided she knew why. Because a woman's grief was something to be borne alone, away from where it would make others uncomfortable.

Violet was openly sobbing now, and the wolves were agitated by her cries. Before, they'd been mostly still, watchful; but they'd turned restless, and were pacing among the trees on the edge of the clearing. One of the creatures soon edged forward from the shadows, came close enough that Helen could hear its breathing.

Helen's people believed there was a sacred connection between themselves and these wild creatures. For a fleeting moment, she wondered if this was a she-wolf; if the animal somehow sensed, and understood, Violet's anguish.

Even so, Helen edged closer to her distraught friend and kept an eye on the rifle in Violet's lap.

"You have to let Amelia go," she whispered to Violet, whose sobs continued to echo through the clearing. Close by, an owl hooted from a low-hanging branch. "Her spirit has moved on from this world. And her body won't be disturbed. That rock keeps it safe."

But even as she spoke, Helen understood why her friend continued to observe these melancholy vigils. If Violet let go of her fears about Amelia's resting place, she'd have to release some of her grief. And even though it weighed her down, like a stone in her heart, Violet simply wasn't ready.

"You sound like Ingrid Kempel," Violet said bitterly. *"Don't worry, dearie, you'll have more."*

All the wolves pricked their ears as Violet mimicked her older neighbor's high-pitched words.

"Why, I myself have had eleven, with just eight left on this side of the earth. But I don't want more babies. I only want Amelia."

Before she even realized what she was doing, Helen placed a protective hand over her own abdomen. Despite the gloom in the clearing, and being buried deep in her own despair, Violet immediately noticed the gesture and knew what it meant.

"Oh, Winona!" Violet was aware of the secret that no one else in Eagle River knew. She quickly set aside her agony to focus on her friend's predicament. "Are you sure? Have you told Pierre?"

Helen shook her head. She hadn't been sure until a few days ago. If she confided in her husband, she wondered, would it make things better, or worse? Sometimes, Helen caught herself hoping that something would go wrong with this pregnancy, like that other time, and it would all be over. But then, she'd cling to the idea of having something, someone, that was truly her own.

Never mind about Pierre. This baby would be all hers, no matter what.

Helen hadn't meant to share this news with Violet so soon. Not when her friend was still grieving this hard, when her grasp on her emotions was so precarious.

"I don't know what I'm going to tell him." She shook her head. "Maybe I'm waiting for some nudge, some sign about what to do. Until then, it'll be our secret."

Violet nodded. "I won't say a word. I promise." She turned her attention back to the predators in their midst, snatching up the lantern and waving it aloft.

"Get back! Leave us alone!" she shouted to the wolves. All five made keening noises, and retreated closer to the trees.

Helen looked down the hill at the village. The skeleton-limbed trees kept most of the homes and Eagle River's few stores tucked inside the shadows. But the twin rails of steel glowed in the moonlight, and she could just make out the hulking shape of the railroad trestle where it crossed the river on the east edge of town.

Other than its plethora of brick buildings, Eagle River was no different than most of the white people's villages.

But oh, how Helen hated this place.

She hated the stares, the whispers. Or, sometimes worse, the way people looked right through her, as if she didn't even exist. How many of them suspected she was living a lie? How many of them had figured out her true situation with Pierre, yet didn't care?

Helen felt so alone in this world, the one created by the white people. Especially now that it seemed she was carrying a child.

She had Violet to talk to, thank goodness; but the incredible changes that were coming made her yearn to confide in someone else, too. Especially when Violet was still reeling from Amelia's death.

Helen thought of Mrs. Baxter, who ran the post office in one corner of the mercantile.

Helen made sure to visit on those afternoons when Lena

was behind the counter, her little boy in a large basket at her feet.

Helen always asked after letters for Pierre. None had arrived, but she still hoped someone would insist her husband take responsibility for the crimes he'd committed.

Lena had noticed Helen's interest in the newspapers that were often stacked on the counter, but the postmaster had quickly figured out the younger woman was merely staring at the illustrations. To Helen's amazement, Lena knew a little French. And now, she was teaching Helen her English letters.

When Pierre wasn't home, Helen studied the old newspapers Lena had given her, then practiced her penmanship in their margins before they were tossed into the fire. The papers were full of news about the war, the one the white people now waged against each other. But there was so much more to read, to learn.

As kind as Lena Baxter was, Helen wasn't convinced she should tell her about the baby. But she knew that learning to read and write English would make it easier to fend for herself and her child.

The wolves had beat a hasty retreat when Violet held her lantern high, but they'd refused to leave the hillside. The creatures' fallback was short-lived, and they seemed determined to regain the ground they'd claimed earlier that night. Violet yelled at them again, ready to defend her post; but the wolves were just as persistent.

This is madness, Helen thought. *Violet can never win this war.*

And then, Helen had an idea. It was a simple one, so obvious that it was hard to believe no one had thought of it before.

Or had they, and not taken action? Helen decided to do just that.

"What we need is a fence," she told Violet. "One with strong iron bars that are too tall for the wolves to get over. It would keep them away from Amelia. Would that help?"

"Yes, oh yes," Violet whispered. "She'd be safe, then. But ... how do we make that happen?"

"I'm going to find a way. Leave it to me."

Mr. Baxter had brought the railroad to Eagle River two years ago, had enough money and power to command miles and miles of wooden timbers and stretches of steel to do his bidding. Surely, he could convince Eagle River's leaders to purchase enough fence to enclose this sacred spot. And Lena, from what Helen knew of her, would eagerly rally her husband to accept such a challenge.

The wolves were still watching, waiting. For what? For Violet to lift her rifle, and fire? For the girls to run?

Helen was tired of running; and she was tired of battling those who fenced her in.

"Are you ready to go home?" she asked Violet, who nodded in agreement.

The idea of a fence had given her grieving friend hope. Even so, Helen knew many more nights would be spent up on this ridge until Amelia's resting place was secure.

"Let's stand up ... slowly," Helen told Violet. "Stare them down. Predators thrive on fear. We need them to know we're not afraid."

As the girls got to their feet, one of the wolves lifted its snout toward the moon and let loose with a long howl. Another quickly did the same, and the pack seemed ready to move. But Violet tipped her rifle in their direction, and the creatures remained clustered near the back of the clearing.

Once Violet and Helen started down the footpath, Helen looked back over her shoulder. The wolves had swiftly moved in, just as she'd suspected they would. They yipped and grunted at each other, relaxed and confident now that they'd regained control of the hillside. While the alpha kept watch, the other four sniffed the ground where the girls had sat and paced around Amelia's grave.

Helen made sure Violet didn't see. She asked Violet about the quilt she was sewing, kept her friend focused on their careful steps through the weeds as the lantern showed them the way back to the wagon road.

* * *

A light was burning in Violet and Joseph's cabin. Helen gave her friend a hug at the yard gate, and vowed to speak to Mrs. Baxter as soon as possible.

And then, as she walked through the dark toward her own home, Helen made another promise. This time, to the baby she carried.

If it thrived, and if it survived its birth, she'd give her own life if necessary to save this new one. And her child would never know fear, or pain, or hunger.

A sharp wind came out of nowhere, it seemed, and whistled among the bare-limbed trees as Helen reached her own yard. She felt the power of the wind, and the strength of her *unci*, and all the others who'd gone before.

Steeled by a new resolve, Helen went inside the cabin and took off her coat. Pierre was snoring now, and the fire burned low.

Nothing else had changed in her absence, but Helen knew she wasn't the same girl who'd left this cabin just hours ago. Once already in her life, she'd changed her name and buried her beliefs to suit someone else, to keep herself safe. She would do it again; she'd shift and grow into whatever was required of her if it meant she could break free.

As she neared the bed, a searing pain suddenly shot from her wrist to her elbow.

"Who you been with?" Pierre's words were slurred, but his grip was as strong as ever.

"No one. Let me go!"

It was the truth. And not only because she hadn't slipped out to meet another man.

Violet was of no interest, of no consequence, to Pierre. She was just another girl; a crazy girl who wandered out of her cabin at night to fraternize with the wolves on the hillside. A silly woman whose husband was too stupid to keep her at home.

Helen finally managed to pull away, and rushed around the bed. It was so close to the wall of their tiny cabin that she had to turn sideways to climb in. Even while she slept, Pierre had her cornered.

She sank into the lumpy corn-husk mattress, and pulled her side of the quilt up to her chin.

Across the river and on the hill, the wolves were howling again. What would it feel like, she wondered, to be that free?

In her mind's eye, Helen saw the ragged grass beneath her bare feet, felt the cool autumn wind on her face, sensed the movement of the pack.

As she closed her eyes, Helen reached down and touched the side seam of her nightgown. Through the thin calico, the solid, comforting shape of her folded knife appeared under her palm. She'd sewn in the hidden pocket only days ago, when it had become apparent that she could be carrying a child. More hiding places had been created in both her petticoats.

Helen would keep her wits about her, and her knife always within reach.

Not all the wolves lived in the forest. If the one sleeping beside her lunged at her again, she would find the courage to strike.

Welcome, Mr. President

* 1876 *

The lilies were pink and white, showy and fragrant; and mere hours from becoming fodder for the waste bin just outside the kitchen door.

Carrie pursed her lips as she snipped the stems' bottoms with her sharpest pair of shears, and nestled the flowers into a clean jar of fresh spring water.

"What a waste," she muttered as she worked. "Only Adam Baxter would order a dozen blooms from some greenhouse out East, and have them shipped out here in this heat."

The lilies had arrived on yesterday's train, nestled in a straw-packed wooden crate that had been wedged between bags of flour. Not all the water had sloshed out of the glass tubes, thank goodness; but a two-day ride in a stifling, dusty railcar was an ordeal these hothouse flowers wouldn't be able to overcome.

Frank, who managed the depot, had brought the flowers home last night. With a beseeching look, he'd pleaded with his wife to work her green-thumb magic.

So, as she always did, Carrie Sonberg had given it a go; and this morning, she'd repeated the process one more time, just in case.

But she sighed as she stepped back to study her work. If the flowers were salvageable, they would have bounced back by now. But the lilies were as limp and wilted as when she'd taken possession of them yesterday.

Two of her younger boys were yelling about something upstairs, but that wasn't anything new. Next came rapid footsteps, then Greta's shriek of dismay.

"Mother, they won't give it back!" echoed down the stairwell. "They just stole my very-best ribbon. What am I going to do with my hair? This is the most important day of the year, and they're ruining it!"

Carrie was too tired, and too overwhelmed, to intervene. She prayed for patience and, please God, if it wasn't too much to ask for, just a few minutes of peace.

But in a house packed full of children, that was about as rare as what would occur this afternoon in Eagle River. At thirteen, Greta was prone to dramatics; but this time, her comment accurately summed up the situation.

President Ulysses S. Grant would arrive in just a few hours. His personal train, a handful of custom cars outfitted with all the comforts of a first-rate hotel, was scheduled to make a stop on its way from Chicago to St. Paul. The entire village had buzzed with anticipation from the moment the visit was announced two weeks ago.

As the wife of the stationmaster, Carrie had been asked to step forward and offer the president a lovely bouquet. Along with Mayor Murphy, Frank and Adam would shake hands with members of the president's entourage as they basked in the glow of their little town's triumph.

Today was Eagle River's moment in the sun, but Carrie couldn't seem to muster up any excitement. Even so, she vowed she wouldn't present these limp, shriveled blooms to the president. Especially when one of Eagle River's best cutting gardens waited right outside her back door.

"I don't care what they cost," she said irritably as she snatched the lilies from the jar. "These will never do! They look like something the cat dragged in."

Marmalade was perched on the wooden chair nestled next to an open kitchen window; it was her favorite spot for keeping tabs on this busy household's comings and goings. As the cat washed her orange face with one white paw, she exuded an air of serenity that Carrie hadn't felt in months, if ever.

"My apologies, Marmie," Carrie said as she started toward the back door. "You have far better taste than that."

She retrieved a basket from beneath the back porch's bench, then rubbed her lower back. Something always seemed to ache these days, even on a warm, sunny June afternoon. And if she wasn't physically uncomfortable, it was all but a certainty that Carrie's thoughts could scatter as quickly as little James tossed his jacks across the floor. Her shifting moods came and went, drifted here and there, like the puffy clouds in the summer sky.

At fifty-one, Carrie knew her life had irrevocably changed. She just didn't know what to think about that, or how best to carry on.

James met her at the edge of the garden, his hands cupped together in an all-too familiar way. What now? Yesterday, it had been a baby robin that had flown its nest too soon.

At nine, James still believed his mother was the wisest woman on the face of the earth. That was going to change in a few years, so Carrie had tried not to scold him too harshly as she'd instructed him to put the little bird back where he'd found it.

"What have you there?" she asked her youngest as she dumped the lilies into the compost bin. James opened his hands just enough to reveal the full-grown frog resting inside.

"Isn't he splendid, Mama? I'm sure he grew up in the little pond behind the stable. Can I take him to the depot and give him to the president?"

Carrie burst out laughing. That would be much more

exciting than a handful of flowers!

"No, no; Freddie the Frog needs to stay here. This is his home." With a shake of her head, she declined James' offer to hold the creature. "Take him back to the pond, then wash up and change your clothes. I don't want us to be late!"

Carrie plucked her cutting shears from her apron pocket as she approached the rows of vibrant flowers along the side of the garden. Many of the women wondered how Carrie found the time and energy to tend to these blooms, especially since the vegetables that made up most of the plot had to be her priority.

The truth was, these flowers had saved Carrie's sanity several times over the years. She could turn the earth, pull weeds, plant new seeds and watch them thrive; it had given her a great deal of satisfaction to create something of beauty.

"Here you are, my lovelies. Who among you is ready to greet the president?"

The peonies had lasted longer than expected this year, so several of the dark pink ones would go into the bouquet. The purple phlox, which were just coming on, would give the bouquet some height. Contrast could come from a scattering of cosmos, perhaps the white and cobalt blue.

It would make a wonderful statement. A spray of fresh, vibrant blooms that would best anything found in some fancy shop miles from Eagle River.

Carrie's mind was much more at ease as she returned to the cool shade of the kitchen. The exclamations of Mary, the Sonbergs' hired girl, proved her hunch had been right.

"That's a smart thing, ma'am," Mary said as she handed Carrie her best hat, which had been cleaned and refreshed with new trim. "There's no better way to show Mr. Grant what we're made of than to give him flowers right out of your own garden! I don't know the president personally; but for myself, lilies make me sneeze."

Carrie laughed. "You are right, as always. We don't want

the president sniffling and gasping for air during his speech." She checked the clock. "I'm going to freshen up, then get over to the depot with the flowers. I know you and Martha will herd the younger children down the street when it's time."

Martha was nineteen, and already catching the eye of many of the town's young men. She had her mother's brown eyes and dark, wavy tresses, but had yet to acquire the portly frame Carrie came face to face with as she stood before her dressing table's mirror.

Some additional girth was to be expected, of course, after so many pregnancies; and Carrie was no longer young. Alice and Gertrude were long ago out of the house and married. Alice had made Carrie a grandmother three times already, and Gertie was expecting her first.

Carrie's hair now had more gray strands than brown, but once her lavender frock was in place and her best hat perched just-so on her head, Carrie decided she was stylish and festive enough for this afternoon's celebration.

On her way down the hall, she rapped lightly on Henry's bedroom door. He was thirty-two, but still lived at home.

"Yeah?" came the sullen prompt from within. Carrie heard a thump, and then another, but the door didn't open. She waited for a moment, but the way into her son's room remained locked.

Just like his heart, sometimes, she thought as she knocked again.

"I hope you'll join us this afternoon," Carrie told the closed door, willing her encouragement to pass through it and reach her son. "This is an important day. Not just for the town, but for your father. He'd really like it if you'd ..."

"I'll be there." But Henry's tone didn't make it clear that he would.

"Martha and Mary and everyone else are leaving at two. Don't worry about your clothes, dear. Just put on whatever is comfortable."

As she lingered in the hallway, Carrie fanned herself with one hand. Frank had designed this house with enough windows to provide cross ventilation in the summer. Every pane upstairs was wide open; how could she be sweating this much?

"Father's not going to parade me around, I hope," Henry said through the door. "I don't have to join the others at the bandstand, do I?"

"Only if you want to. There will be a crowd, as it is."

Carrie waited, but Henry didn't respond. She hurried downstairs and reached for the flowers, which Mary had tied with a length of leftover blue ribbon and tucked into a water-filled vase.

With a few parting words of thanks to the hired girl, Carrie walked out into the bright sunshine.

* * *

Between President Grant's impending visit and the United States' centennial, many of Hartland County's residents were awash in a wave of nostalgia these days. As she set out for the train station, Carrie pondered how much things had changed since she'd arrived in Eagle River.

The community was not yet twenty years old, but had grown greatly in size and importance during that time. The same could be said for the Sonberg family. Their initial investment in the railroad, as well as Frank being a not-so-silent partner in the mill, meant they lived in relative comfort. Their current house, a two-story red brick with limestone trim, was a great improvement from the cramped cabin that had been their first home in this village.

The houses on this stretch of Oakland Avenue were similar in size, whether built of the town's trademark bricks or clad in narrow clapboards with smart white trim.

Down the way, she caught a glimpse of the Bradfords' new home that was still under construction. Designed in the

Queen Anne style, it was ornate and impressive, if a little much for Carrie's simple tastes.

The Baxters were also planning to build a new house next year. Adam had founded the town's only bank a few years ago; and that, coupled with his longtime investments in the railroad, made him the richest man in town.

Along with scores of new residents, the community had attracted several competent tradesmen since the end of the Civil War. Eagle River now had several dry goods stores, two millinery shops, and a farm-implement dealer with a showroom full of shiny plows and harnesses.

Along with the bank, it boasted an insurance agent, a blacksmith, a newspaper office, and several more services. The mill continued to prosper on the north end of town; the brick kiln on the far-south end, down along the river, had expanded into what could rightly be described as a factory.

Situated along a river and bisected by a railroad line, Eagle River had become more than Frank, Adam, and the other founders ever could have dreamed was possible. Except for one thing. Despite being the first town platted in Hartland County and its initial county seat, Eagle River's location in the far northeast corner had become less convenient as more settlers arrived.

Swanton, twenty miles to the west and south, sprang up quickly after the Civil War. Even though it didn't secure a railroad line until 1868, a county-wide vote in 1870 saw Swanton named the new seat of government.

An elaborate courthouse was now under construction there to replace the clapboard structure that currently housed the county offices.

Many had assumed Grant's locomotive would pass through Swanton on its way to Minnesota's capital, Saint Paul; but somehow, Eagle River received that nod. Truth be told, Carrie wasn't surprised when the route was announced.

Adam Baxter wasn't exactly shady; Carrie had known

him for almost two decades, and had yet to unearth any evidence of illegal doings on his part.

But she was certain Adam had leveraged his considerable influence to make sure the president's personal train stopped in Eagle River instead.

Residents from across the region had started to arrive not long after sunrise. Mary had reported that Main Street, whose businesses were festooned with patriotic bunting, was packed with wagons and carriages as visitors darted in and out of the shops. Attendees would enjoy their picnic lunches in the shade of the town's grand oak trees, then follow the president's procession from the depot to the town park.

As she walked toward Second Street, Carrie heard the municipal band tuning up at the bandstand. While the specifics of the president's address weren't known, Carrie was certain it would champion the virtues of this great country, then praise the industrious spirit of Hartland County's residents. Of course, the unlimited potential of America's bright future was sure to be mentioned, as well.

Because President Grant was once General Grant, organizers had put out a call for Hartland County's veterans to attend the ceremony and receive recognition for their bravery during the Civil War. The event was to be a "moving and patriotic moment, a true display of Hartland County's grit and resilience," according to the breathless article in last week's newspaper.

Perhaps. But for Carrie, the idea of such a ceremony made her heart ache with longing and loss. The war had been over for a decade, but the scars it had left on this community and its families had yet to fade.

Henry had been barely eighteen when he'd run off to fight. A year and a half later, he'd come home missing most of his right leg.

He occasionally worked at the depot; but it was more charity than anything, Henry told his mother, spurred by

Father's guilt that his job as a railroad stationmaster had exempted him from the draft.

Several of the other local boys had also been injured; a few of them were amputees like Henry. Even so, many of the wounded had married and started families of their own. But Henry seemed to have given up on life, and Carrie feared the day she'd find her son dead by his own hand.

He drank too much; even Frank thought so. And too many nights, Carrie rushed to her now-grown son's room to put her arms around him as he screamed and shouted at the phantoms that stalked him in his sleep.

When Henry had been a boy, she'd often climbed the ladder to their cabin's loft to ease his fears about the wolves and panthers that wandered the village after dark. These days, nothing Carrie said seemed to calm her troubled son.

But the thing that haunted Henry the most, she knew, wasn't the loss of his leg. Nor was it the subsequent loss of his youth. It was the loss of George.

One of Carrie's heels caught the edge of the wooden sidewalk along Second Street, and she took a moment to regain her balance. The sun suddenly seemed too bright, despite the fashionably wide brim of her hat. Tears filled her eyes, even as she tried to blink them away.

With the vase of flowers still in her hand, Carried ducked under the massive canopy of the ancient maple tree just off the corner. She leaned back, not caring if the rough bark wrinkled her best dress, and closed her eyes.

George would be thirty-four, if he'd lived. If he hadn't fallen on the battlefield at Vicksburg, shot in the shoulder. If the surgeons had moved fast enough to remove the musket ball, if the infection hadn't spread ...

Her firstborn, her oldest son, was gone.

George had been drafted when he was twenty; it was the reason Henry had insisted on volunteering. The world had viewed their boys as men, and Frank and Carrie hadn't been able to stop either of them from leaving.

The brothers had served side by side for over a year, Carrie's only comfort that they were at least together. Even, and especially, at the end. That George hadn't died alone, that Henry had been there with him.

George had been buried in Vicksburg, a place so far away that Carrie had never been able to see it for herself. All that remained of George was a cherished photo, the few pieces of clothing he'd left at home, an empty chair at the table, and the words of love he deputized Henry to share with their family once he made it home to Eagle River.

And today, just like all the other left-behind mothers and wives and sweethearts, Carrie would be expected to cheer and applaud. To bask in the glory of the North's victory, and the country's healing. As the wife of the stationmaster, Carrie's smile was expected to be twice as wide, her words of welcome twice as gracious.

How was she ever going to get through it?

Carried took a few deep breaths, then rejoined the crowds making their way toward the depot. It was wonderfully dim and cool inside the station, despite the dozens of people milling about. Either they were looking for their friends in the throng, or eager to purchase a cup of lemonade from the ladies' aid society.

Like so many others across the country, the local organization had formed during the war to send donated supplies to the soldiers. Since then, the club had expanded its mission to aid less-fortunate members of the community.

Before Carrie could even adjust her hat, Lena Baxter appeared at her elbow. Although Lena was a decade younger than Carrie, they were close friends.

"Let me guess; the lilies didn't make it?" Lena let out a low chuckle. "I told Adam it was a fool's errand, but he didn't listen. These are beautiful! I'm just sorry you had to carry them down here in this heat."

Lena's husband soon appeared out of the crowd. His blonde hair carried a touch of gray these days, although he tried his best to hide it. Carrie had never met a man as vain, or as ambitious, as Adam Baxter.

Before Adam could get a word in, Lena explained about the lilies and noted how these beautiful, homegrown flowers were sure to impress the president. She then waited with a small smile while her husband tried to hide his disappointment.

"I suppose they will be fine," he finally said. "I've heard the White House is filled with lilies; Mrs. Grant is such an admirer of flowers. I thought ..."

Lena gave Carrie's shoulder a supportive squeeze, then gave her a chance to escape. "How about you take them into Frank's office? They may need a bit more water on a day like today."

Frank's office was empty, thank goodness. Carrie shut the door behind her, and placed the vase on a corner of her husband's neatly arranged desk.

Her buoyant mood from those peaceful moments in her garden was long gone. Her temples had started to throb, and her throat was dry. A water pitcher waited nearby on a small table; Carrie poured some for the flowers, then filled a glass for herself.

The blooms had shifted during their trip to the depot. She set the blue ribbon aside and lifted the stems this way and that, tried to rebalance the arrangement so the peonies and the phlox were evenly mixed. But no matter what she did, the bouquet didn't look right. There were too many types of flowers, too many colors. What had looked so lovely at home, in her own garden, now seemed showy and fussy.

Maybe Adam was right; the lilies would have been better. Classic, sophisticated. Not a handful of flowers from a prairie garden off a dirt-packed alley. But what else was she going to do? The president's train was supposed to arrive in less than an hour. And Carrie had no doubt that Grant would be right on time.

Adam's frown of disappointment flashed through Carrie's whirling thoughts. He'd looked like a little boy whose favorite toy had gone missing. Were these flowers really that important? If Lena hadn't been there, hadn't stepped in, Carrie might have given that man a piece of her mind.

And Frank, yesterday evening ... her dear Frank; always so patient, so kind. He'd handed her the crate of languishing lilies with so much despair on his face, but despair mixed with hope. Not unlike the expression little James had worn when he'd shown his mother the baby robin.

Because Carrie would know exactly what to do. She would take care of it, whatever it was. Find a solution, raise everyone's spirits ...

"Just like everything else I've fixed over the years." Carrie jostled the flowers back and forth, the heat rising in her face.

"I've had to make do with whatever's been tossed at me. This town, our family, our home ... but I can't work miracles! Why does everyone expect me to do exactly that?"

Suddenly, Carrie was filled with rage. She was tired of deferring to the expectations placed upon her, of constantly having to find ways to smooth life's sharp edges for everyone else.

And nothing that she might ever accomplish in life, or anything that would happen on this historic day in Eagle River, was going to heal her broken son. Or bring her dead one home.

Not the rousing speeches, or the joyful tunes from the band. Not even President Grant himself.

A war hero, indeed. What about George? He'd made the ultimate sacrifice to mend this torn-apart country.

The generals, on both sides, had spent most of their time loitering in their fancy tents, surrounded by their aides. They'd played cards, sipped coffee, and gulped whiskey while both of Carrie's sons and hundreds of thousands of other men had lain on the battlefields, wounded, gasping for breath and screaming in pain ...

Carrie's hands were shaking. She stepped away from the vase of flowers, so she wouldn't lift it up and smash it into pieces on the floor. Both office windows were open, and she ran to the closest one and breathed in the fresh air.

Footsteps echoed on the other side of the office door. The latch clicked, and Frank appeared. Behind his spectacles, his brown eyes were full of concern.

She must look a fright, Carrie decided, and her hands instinctively went to the brim of her hat and the hairpins below it. But she didn't care.

"My dear, what has happened?" Frank closed the door, reached her in three quick steps, and put his arms around her. "I know Adam's disappointed about the flowers, but he'll get over it. Everything else ..."

"I don't give a damn about those flowers!" Carrie was almost shouting; it felt good. "I also don't give a damn about the president! Who does he think he is?"

Her husband took a small step back. "He's our leader," Frank said slowly. "A great man, deserving of every honor that can be bestowed upon him. Why are you so upset?"

Carrie tried to find the words. Years of resentment, of heartache, flowed through her mind. And then, she made a decision. It was a small one. But it was something that no one, not even her husband, could force her to reconsider.

"I won't do it!" she told Frank. "I'm not going to stand there, simpering, with those flowers in my hands, and welcome Mr. Grant to our fair town."

She gave a rueful laugh. "Besides, why are you asking a grown woman to take on a little girl's errand? Do you want me to drop a curtsy, while I'm at it? He's not royalty; and I wouldn't care if he was."

"But you have to. I promised Adam that ..."

"That's right! You did." She pointed at her husband. "You didn't ask me, did you? Just assumed I'd do it, that I'd go along with whatever the two of you cooked up."

Frank checked the clock. "Why are you doing this now? The president will be here soon. What are we supposed to do? Carrie, why are you so angry?"

"You know why." Carrie began to pace the floor. "Or maybe, you don't. But you should. It's Ulysses S. Grant's fault that George is gone, and Henry is the way he is. Oh, it's not all his doing, I know; but enough of it falls on his shoulders. I want nothing to do with that man, today or any other day."

Frank was clearly flustered. "Lower your voice, please. If anyone hears ..."

Carrie raised it, instead. "I don't care! And I want Grant to feel what I feel! What all of us mothers and wives and daughters have felt, for years. Our men, taken away for good. Or sent back to us as strangers. The war never really ended for us."

Frank blinked, then looked at his feet.

"And you," Carrie said to her husband, "why don't you say his name, anymore? He was our son, Frank. Our dear George, who's never coming home."

She waited while Frank turned away to stare out the window.

"I miss him, too," he finally said. "I haven't forgotten about George. And every day, to see how Henry suffers .... but nothing I can say, or do, will change anything."

And then, he gently placed his hands on his wife's shoulders. "Carrie, listen to me. I know you're upset."

She rolled her eyes.

"No, listen." Frank's voice was barely above a whisper. "Give it an hour. Then you can head home, have a nice bath. Don't bother coming to the park afterward, if you're not up to it. You don't have to mingle around. I'll tell the others you're not feeling well. But you need to do this. And it's so easy."

He gestured at the flowers, still so cheerful despite the heat.

"All you have to do is hold them out, put on a smile, and say: 'Welcome, Mr. President.' That's it. It's one moment, dear. Just one moment, and then you can go."

He waited. Carrie waited.

"No," she said.

The office door popped open again. It was Lena, with Harriet Fagan in tow. Harriet was the president of the ladies' aid society.

"Oh," Lena said in surprise. "Sorry to interrupt." She frowned with concern at Carrie's tear-streaked face. "Is everything OK?"

"I'm not going to do it." Carrie spoke before Frank could. "I'm not about to hand a bunch of flowers, or anything else, to Grant. He, and his kind, are the reason George is dead and Henry is no longer himself. I don't care if he's the president. I want nothing to do with this, with any of it."

There was a pause, as if the depot itself was holding its breath.

Lena Baxter was a formidable woman; educated, intelligent, and sometimes the only person who could keep her willful husband on the right track. And as one of Carrie's closest friends, she knew all of Carrie's struggles and disappointments.

"Then you shouldn't," Lena said as Frank gasped in surprise and Carrie restated her case.

"It's more than a mother should have to bear," Lena told Frank. "My boys were too young to be called up. And I've thanked the Lord countless times over the years that they were spared."

Lena gestured toward the depot lobby, and the station platform beyond. "Isn't it enough that half the county is here? That there are going to be speeches, and the band, and ice cream? Quite honestly, I don't know why I hadn't thought of it before. Carrie, this is so difficult for you. I'm sorry."

Frank gave Harriet a hopeful look.

"I'm not interested," she told him curtly. "Don't forget, Frank Sonberg, that my Charlie never came home from that terrible war." She dabbed at her eyes with an embroidered handkerchief, then crushed it in an angry fist.

"Philip is as bad as the rest of you men. For weeks, he's been acting as if God himself is going to appear in Eagle River, step down from above, and bestow his blessings upon us."

"I can't believe this." Frank was stunned. "And Harriet, you're the president of the ladies' aid society!"

"Exactly. I plan the Decoration Day service at the cemetery every year. And I started the fundraising drive for that monument in the park, among other things." She gave Carrie an understanding nod. "A mother's work is never done, they say. But we all need a day off, now and then."

Carrie took a deep breath and looked at her friends. How lucky she was to have them! She couldn't help but feel a bit sorry for Frank, as it was clear her husband was struggling with what to say next, what to do.

And then, as she often did, Lena stepped in.

"I have an idea. I think I know of the perfect person to take Carrie's place."

* * *

Adam Baxter impatiently shifted his weight from one foot to the other. All these weeks of planning, all the favors he'd called in to make this happen. What a beautiful day it was! And the crowds! He'd hoped for an impressive turnout, but hadn't expected this.

A loud, long whistle echoed from the east, and the people soon crowded five deep along the railroad tracks, waved their flags, and began to cheer.

The gleaming locomotive chugged over the river trestle,

then slowed to a stop in front of the depot.

The town band launched into a rousing rendition of "The Battle Hymn of the Republic" as the first of the president's assistants appeared on the balcony of his custom coach. Next came several security guards, the brass buttons on their uniforms glowing in the summer sun.

Carrie's homegrown bouquet was rather nice, Adam had to admit as he waited with Frank and Ambrose Murphy, Eagle River's mayor, for President Grant to appear.

It was a shame Carrie had taken ill so suddenly, and was going to miss this historic celebration. She had seemed to be in fine form when she'd arrived; but then, Adam had long ago given up trying to understand women and their complicated ways.

Lena had taken charge of the situation. Adam had hesitated, at first. He was supposed to shake the president's hand, for goodness' sake. His wife gently reminded Adam that he still possessed two of those (unlike Will Taylor, who'd returned from the war in a far-less fortunate state) and he could accomplish both tasks while employing his usual charm.

Of course, there was that other matter that tugged at Adam's conscience as the president stepped out from under the awning of his coach and made his way down the train car's metal steps.

During the war, any man who'd paid the $300 commutation fee was exempt from the draft. Adam hadn't had a problem finding the cash to pay another man to take his place at the front. Clem Bradford had done the same.

Frank would have as well, Adam suspected, if his stationmaster role hadn't prevented his name from appearing on a draft card.

A rich man's war, and a poor man's fight, some had called the War Between the States. Well, maybe that was true. But Adam had been needed at home; he was Eagle River's mayor during that dark time. Someone had to keep this town on the tracks while so many of the other men were away. He'd done his duty, hadn't he?

President Grant had now reached the station platform. He was taller than Adam had expected, and his power and intelligence were palpable as he waved to the crowd.

How amazing it was to be in the presence of this formidable leader! One day, Adam would be able to tell his grandchildren he'd been the very-first person in Eagle River to greet the great man on his once-in-a-lifetime visit to their town.

Clutching the flowers in his left hand, Adam stepped forward before Frank, or even Ambrose, could beat him to it. He offered a dazzling smile, a quick nod that he hoped conveyed both pride and deference, and held out the bouquet.

"Welcome, Mr. President," he said.

Americans

* 1899 *

The chicken soup Sarah had made this Friday night wasn't the usual. She watched her elderly father's face out of the corner of her eye as she put the steaming pot on the kitchen table, a towel protecting the oilcloth underneath.

"*Was ist das*?" Levi's white eyebrows knitted together in confusion as he leaned forward from his place at the head of the table. "Where is the *knoedel*? Your mother would be very disappointed."

While the rest of the family almost always spoke English, even at home, her father still seasoned his conversations with hearty sprinkles of the German he'd known all his life.

"I ran out of time, Papa! We've been very busy down at the store, with that big sale going on this week. And you know how much work those dumplings can be."

Actually, he didn't; Sarah was certain her father's kitchen skills did not go beyond making a sandwich. That was women's work.

"The noodles are just as good," she told him. "I had extra already prepared from a few nights ago. And I know you like them."

Levi dipped his chin; his daughter was right. He could eat homemade noodles several nights a week.

Sarah turned back to the stove, and added more wood

from the box. This building on Eagle River's Main Street was only twelve years old, with red brick on the outside and heavily plastered walls on the inside. Even so, the February cold seemed to creep in around every window frame and through every corner.

She paused for a moment to listen for the sound of her husband's and son's footsteps in the building's back stairwell. None yet. It was just as well; she might have time to sweep the kitchen floor before dinner.

"The sale is why Sam and Isaac are running late," she told Levi as she reached for the broom. "And we don't close until six on Fridays, as you know. They have to tidy up to be ready for tomorrow. Saturday is the busiest time of the week. And Sam always likes to square the ledger at the end of the day."

"It's Shabbat!" Levi hissed. He gestured toward the darkness outside the kitchen's two windows, which looked over the back lots of Main Street. "Friday night, all of Saturday; no working, no counting money ..." He shook his head in disgust. "The store is open for nine hours on Saturdays. Nine hours! Back home, we'd be cast out, shunned for such shocking behavior."

Sarah's broom jerked to a stop, and her eyes darted anxiously toward the front of their apartment. The lilting strains of a popular waltz drifted down the long hallway from the sitting room. Eva and Rebecca, in a fit of Friday-night restlessness, had picked out a cylinder for the phonograph and cranked it to life.

"Keep your voice down," she admonished Levi. "You know the rules, Papa. Thank goodness the girls just put on some music."

Sarah put her free hand on her hip. "You like to eat, yes? And be warm? Where did those shoes on your feet come from? That store provides everything we need, gives us a comfortable life. One that we never could have dreamed of back home."

Sarah was determined to shield her two youngest children from their family's biggest secret, but she also understood that the situation was harder on her father than anyone else. Levi had long been at the advanced age where people looked back far more than they looked forward. It would make sense that he was homesick for the Old Country, as his memories of his tough life there had been softened by time.

Sarah put the broom back in the corner, and took her seat at the table. "Now, Papa," she said more kindly, "I know this is tough for you. Our life here in Eagle River is … very different. And it's not what you'd expected, at the end of your life."

"Am I dying, then?" He crossed his arms. "That new young doctor; did he tell you that, when I wasn't listening?" Levi sat up straighter with a sarcastic grin. "My hearing's as sharp as ever. Don't think you can fool me."

"You're healthy as a horse, and I'm glad." Sarah leaned in close. "But Papa, I need you to stop talking like that. Talking about the old ways. Especially around the girls. When we left New York fifteen years ago, we made a decision, remember? We were happy to have you join us here, but that was part of the bargain we made."

"You mean that Sam made," Levi muttered.

Sarah bit back her frustration. How many times must they have this conversation?

"It was my choice, too. Isaac only remembers a little here and there, and he's old enough to understand how important it is to leave the past in the past." She gestured around them. "But this is all the girls know. And it is all they will ever know."

Levi sighed, then finally nodded.

"I don't agree that it's better to be Methodist, but I was outvoted." At least he was keeping his voice down now. "But I still don't understand the part about your last name. What was wrong with Schneider? It sounds just as German as it does Jewish, and this town is full of Germans, anyway. Why does it need to be Sherwood? That's more English than anything, if you ask me."

Sarah asked God, whichever version might be answering her prayers these days, to grant her patience.

"We decided that it was *safer* to be Methodist," she reminded her father, "not necessarily better. That's what the Feldmans did, before they came here."

"But the Feldmans didn't change their name. They're still the Feldmans, last I heard."

Nearly twenty years ago, the Feldmans had lived in the same Lower Manhattan tenement at the Schneiders and worked for the same sweatshop managers. The Feldmans had owned a butcher shop back in Germany, but had found too many butchers already established in their Jewish New York neighborhood.

With distant family members already settled in this part of Iowa, the Feldmans decided to move west for the fresh air and better employment opportunities. Their Eagle River butcher shop had never been kosher, of course; but it was profitable from its early days on. So much so, they'd invited the Schneiders to join them.

Sam was the one to suggest they change their last name when they moved to Eagle River, and Sarah had been surprised to find she didn't mind in the least. It was a clean slate all around, a fresh start.

Maybe it was easier for her because she'd already changed her surname once, when she married Sam. Giving up her native religion had been harder, of course. But she still believed that choice had opened the door to a better life for her children. And that was all that mattered.

"We are still ourselves," she told her father, "no matter what we call ourselves. And besides," she added with a laugh as she got up from her chair, "you're not a Sherwood; never will be."

"Thank goodness for that." Levi reached for a slice of the still-warm bread that waited on the table, and Sarah didn't stop him. Isaac and Sam were especially late tonight; it would be best to put the soup back on the stove until they came up from the store.

"But if we're not Jewish anymore, and never will be," her father said in a near-whisper around a mouthful of fresh bread, "why do you bother honoring Shabbat with our Friday-night suppers?"

"Because the soup is delicious; Grandma's recipe never disappoints. It's comfort food, it feeds the soul. And besides, more snow is coming tomorrow."

The phonograph in the front room had changed its tune again. This time, the girls had put on one of those ragtime recordings Isaac had purchased with some of his wages. Sarah didn't understand this new art form; how did one dance to something that didn't always keep a steady beat?

The phonograph had been Sam's one extravagant purchase after he'd closed the books on 1897. He'd justified it as an anniversary present of sorts, as that year had marked a decade since the Sherwoods had opened their own store.

Sam and Sarah had helped the Feldmans run their butcher shop, still just down the street, for a few years when they'd first arrived in Eagle River. With the money they'd saved, they put a down payment on this building when the block was redeveloped from a scattering of clapboard stores into this tight row of grand brick structures.

Business at the Sherwoods' mercantile had been busy from the start; three years ago, they'd paid off the loan.

Maybe these buildings weren't all that grand, Sarah decided as she started down the hall, but they seemed that way to her. It was a whole twenty steps from the kitchen to the spacious front sitting room, and she passed a bathroom with running water on her way. Her father had a small room of his own right off the kitchen; and then, front to back, the other half of the apartment had three rooms for Sarah and Sam, then Isaac, and Rebecca and Eva.

All of it was a world away from the cramped homes and meager plots of land Sam's and Sarah's families had known in Germany. When her extended family had arrived in New York City, they'd found a vibrant neighborhood filled with other Jews, just as promised.

But they also had to crowd almost a dozen people into their apartment's two small, dark rooms. The sewing machines took up so much space that there was hardly room for the beds. Pallets were rolled out on the floor for the children once the workday was done.

The tenement was by turns suffocatingly hot, and freezing cold; the building reeked with the stench of garbage and human waste. There were too many people huddled in confined spaces, and not enough fresh air. And the fabric lint from their piecework sewing was everywhere no matter how often Sarah, her sister, and their mother cleaned.

Some nights, all these years later, Sarah still woke with a start, certain she could feel the scratchy fibers in her throat and lungs.

Her mother, Rachel, caught consumption during that last winter in the tenements, and her illness was worsened by the poor air. Sarah had taken her turns at her mother's bedside, tried to spoon broth into Rachel's mouth while her mother coughed blood from her ravaged lungs.

Isaac was only five when his grandmother passed. The very next day, Sarah had realized she was pregnant with Eva. The next week, a letter from Eagle River arrived with an offer from the Feldmans that the Schneiders didn't want to turn down. It was time to go.

So much good, so many blessings, had come from that fateful decision. But one thing still hurt Sarah's heart, fifteen years later.

Her sister, Hannah, and her husband had bristled against

the Schneiders' plan, and refused to give up so much of their identity to leave. It was a terrible break that Sarah had yet to repair, one greatly complicated by their father's decision to follow the Schneiders to Iowa. Hannah's letters had arrived less and less as the years went by, until they'd stopped altogether.

Sarah sometimes felt like a spider that had shed its shell several times over. Each season of her life had offered a new way forward. But always, always there was something she'd had to give up, to leave behind.

The sight of her two girls dancing and laughing in the sitting room reminded Sarah that while her choices had been hard, they'd been the right ones. It had been worth it, all of it, to give all three of her children the opportunities they now enjoyed.

Eva and Rebecca had rolled back the rug so they could spin easily on the hardwood floor, and their faces were filled with joy. Outside the three tall windows of the sitting room, the new gas streetlights had flickered on along Main Street, and a few snowflakes tapped at the glass.

"Girls, we'll be eating dinner soon." Sarah pointed at the clock on the side wall, which was about to chime six-thirty. "When this song is over, you'll need to put the rug back where it was."

"Yes, Mama!" Rebecca promised, then squealed with delight as her older sister made another twirl. "Show me, Eva! How did you do that part with your hands?"

As Sarah turned away, she heard a second male voice in the kitchen. Isaac had come up from the store, which meant Sam shouldn't be far behind.

The sprightly music drifting back from the front room must have been infectious, as Isaac grabbed his mother's hand and gave her a spin before he pecked her on the cheek. "Hello, Ma!"

"Goodness!" Sarah laughed. "Had a good day, did you? I

haven't seen you since lunch; I was in the storeroom all afternoon."

Isaac was twenty now, and he'd worked as hard as his father and mother to make their business such a success.

"You could say that, I suppose." Isaac was grinning from ear to ear. "I've made a decision. I've already talked to Pa, and he's given his blessing." Isaac paused long enough to drum his palms on the kitchen table. "I'm going to ask Millie to marry me!"

Sarah let out a whoop of joy; Millie and Isaac had been an item for almost a year. She had hoped for this very thing; but had tried to give her son some privacy, not ask too many questions. He was a grown man now, after all.

"That's wonderful! Oh, Isaac, I'm so happy for you. I mean," Sarah quickly added with a sideways grin, "I'm assuming you're confident she will say yes."

"Millie Crenshaw?" Levi's surprise was colored by a bit of confusion. "You mean to marry her?"

Isaac laughed. "Why, of course! Come on now, Grandpa, don't act as if you don't think the world of her. I seem to recall she charmed you the first time she came over for dinner." He turned toward his mother. "I'd like to give her Grandma Rachel's ring, if I can. I could buy another one, of course, but it wouldn't be as meaningful."

Sarah noticed how silent Levi had become. His weathered hands now gripped the edge of the kitchen table. "Papa, this is a very big day for Isaac. Aren't you excited?"

"She's a lovely girl," Levi told his grandson. "But are you sure she's right for you?"

"I've never been more certain of anything in my life." Isaac's grin dimmed a degree or two as he noticed his grandfather's stern expression and the sudden concern on his mother's face.

"I suppose I had hoped for ... more." Levi's last word hung in the air, like the steam from the still-simmering soup that was back on the stove. "I mean, that maybe you'd decide to ..."

There was a terrible moment of silence. Then another.

"Find a nice Jewish girl, you mean?" Isaac's words came out as a whisper, but the edge of anger in them made Sarah take a step back. Just in time, she remembered not to steady herself by putting a hand on the hot stove. If only Sam would hurry ...

Isaac edged around the table to stare down his grandfather. "I can't believe you just said that!" He was shouting now. "We're Methodist!"

"No, we're Jewish!" Levi hissed.

"We're *Americans*! Or at least, I am." The veins bulged in Isaac's neck, and a fire Sarah rarely saw flared in her son's eyes. "I don't know what you are calling yourself these days. But I was born here; not in some barnyard, back in the Old Country!"

The fury on Levi's face was plain to see. Isaac was a man now, but Levi was still his elder. Insults would not be tolerated.

"That's enough!" Sarah stepped between her son and her father. "Both of you; stop it!"

Then a terrible thought occurred to her. "You don't want the girls to hear!"

To Sarah's surprise, Isaac gave a wry laugh.

"Would that be such a bad thing, really?" At least he'd lowered his voice. "How will you manage to keep them in the dark for the rest of their lives? Someday, Ma, they are going to find out. They might as well know the truth."

"One minute you're turning your back on us," Levi spat out. "The very next, you're embracing your heritage. Which is it? You need to pick a side."

That challenge was directed at her son; even so, her father's comment felt like an arrow to Sarah's heart.

She was the one who had to choose.

Both of them were staring at her now. Her father, with

only a few years left in his long life, and married to tradition. Her son, the heir to their family's name and the booming business downstairs, with so many decades of life ahead of him.

And then, Sarah reminded herself that she'd already made that choice fifteen years ago.

Even so, this was a defining moment in her family's history. If Isaac married Millie (and oh, she hoped he would!) there would be no turning back. Millie's family was Methodist; but it wouldn't have mattered to Sarah if the girl had been Lutheran, or Catholic, or even nothing at all. As long as there was love between Millie and Isaac, she couldn't care less.

But Millie wasn't Jewish, and never would be. Nor would their children, or grandchildren. It would be the same for Eva and Rebecca's descendants. It all ended here and now; on a Friday night in February, in the kitchen above their store.

Levi looked so sad, so defeated, as if he'd aged years in the few minutes he'd argued with his grandson.

Even though she tried to stop them, tears welled up in Sarah's eyes. She was glad for Isaac, of course; but there was another feeling, too. A sense of loss that she'd never expected to feel again, especially all these years later.

"You may have your grandmother's ring," Sarah told her son, even as she expected Levi to mount a rebuttal. But he stayed silent. "I want you to marry Millie, and I want both of you to be happy."

"Thanks, Ma." Isaac hugged her again while Levi merely stared at the table's oilcloth, as if lost in his thoughts. Isaac noticed, too. He swallowed hard; and then his face brightened, just a bit.

"I've been saving up, as you know. We can rent a house, at first, and then ..."

"Rent a house?" It was Sarah's turn to be shocked by her son's plans. "Why, we have plenty of room here for the two of you! At least, for a while. Until the babies start to arrive, or even after ..."

"Ma." Isaac put his hands on her shoulders. Sometimes, she forgot how tall he'd grown. "Millie and I want our own home. We've talked about it already." And then he laughed. "I think the days of this family sleeping 'three to a bed and more on the floor' are long over."

He remembers that? Sarah thought. And then, *of course he does.*

Isaac had been five when they'd left the tenements behind, old enough to recall a thing or two. Somehow, the fact that her son carried a few memories of their old life gave Sarah a bit of comfort. As if all wasn't totally lost.

And maybe someday, when things were much different, when the divide between the past and the future wasn't so sharp, so dangerous, Isaac might share what he knew with some of those to come.

"I've asked around a bit," Isaac said with a light of excitement in his eyes. "It sounds like the old Boucher place is coming up for rent in July. It's small, but the rent will be cheap. We can certainly afford it."

"Oh, no." Levi shook his head and looked at his daughter in dismay. Here, Sarah decided, was one thing they could agree on.

"You don't want to live there," Levi told his grandson. "That place is *heimgesucht*! Boucher's spirit roams that land, has for almost forty years."

Sarah wasn't sure if she believed the rumors about the Boucher place. But she did know that the former cabin, which had been expanded over the years and was now covered in wood siding, had a strange air about it.

Pierre Boucher had been found by his neighbors one morning, everyone said, slumped over his rough-hewn table with a bowl of half-eaten, congealed porridge at his elbow and a sticky spoon at his feet. His young wife was missing, along with their team of horses, their wagon, their cow, and most of their possessions from both inside and outside the cabin.

Pierre had been a violent man, Sarah had also heard, and no one had really believed him when he'd claimed his wife was French. She was a Native American girl, and some of the women had suspected she was with child just weeks before whatever happened inside their cabin. With no signs of obvious injury, and no sign of his wife anywhere, the villagers had simply buried Boucher up on the hillside ... inside the cemetery's new iron fence.

"So, what are you saying?" Isaac was now teasing his grandfather. "Is this Boucher fellow a *dybbuk*? If he was going to take over a living person's body, I'd think he'd have done it by now."

A small smile played at the corner of Levi's mouth. "Shhh. Don't say that word out loud."

Neither of them was about to apologize, that was obvious. But perhaps, the worst had blown over.

"Hopefully, you can find a better place," Sarah told her son. "You have some time."

"Sure, I'll keep looking. But there aren't enough places to rent in this town. People are moving here; and there are young folks like us, just starting out. That's had me thinking: I'd like us to bring in more furniture for the store. It would make us stand out from the competition. People don't want to order everything from a catalog these days; they want to see the pieces in person."

It was an idea Isaac had first mentioned about a year ago. Sam wasn't quite on board, not yet; but both he and Sarah knew their son's ingenuity would be a great asset to the store's future.

"But it's not just that." Isaac pressed on. "What if we turned this whole big upstairs into smaller apartments someday? Maybe two, or three." He pointed this way and that. "It would bring in more income."

"And where would we live?" Sarah asked with a smile. "Or would you be our landlord?"

"Oh, you'll have your own house, someday," Isaac promised. "Just like us."

A house! Sarah could only imagine what that would be like. What would she and Sam do with all that room? And there would be a yard, a garden ...

Boots sounded on the back stairs, and Sam soon appeared in the kitchen. "Well," he said to his son, "I take it you've shared your good news?"

"He sure did," Levi said. It took him a bit of effort, in more ways than one, but he rose to his feet and shook his grandson's hand. "Congratulations, Isaac."

There was still a hint of sadness behind her father's smile, but Levi hid it as best as he could. While he was stubborn, he knew when he'd been defeated.

Sarah let out a breath she hadn't known she was holding. And then, she realized with a start, the phonograph was no longer playing in the front of the apartment.

How long ago had it gone silent? Were the girls still up there? Or were they now in their bedroom, on the other side of the kitchen wall?

And, most importantly ... what had they heard?

"Girls, it's time to eat!" she called in as cheerful of a voice as she could muster. The snow was flying fast and thick now outside the kitchen windows. "The soup's ready."

Secrets always find their way to the light, Sarah's mother had always said. As she turned away from the men's animated conversation to lift the soup pot from the stove, Sarah considered her options. She needed to have a long talk with Sam as soon as possible; they would have to figure out what to do, what to say.

It wouldn't be the first time. But it was going to be the hardest one yet.

One Last Song

✳ 1921 ✳

The applause and whistles echoed in Clara's ears as she made her way backstage. As soon as the tattered velvet curtains fell closed behind her, she yanked off her headband and ran her fingers through her nape-short auburn hair. No matter how she tried to smooth her strands, the humidity in this roadhouse on a steamy August night always brought back the curls.

"Great set, doll." Jake took a drag of his smoke, then offered her a puff. She wasn't about to turn him down; only one was left in her own pack.

"You sure get them boys riled up! But that's just how I like them. They're quick to reach for another drink to put out their thirst after you give them a show."

Clara snorted, and almost dared to blow smoke in the manager's face. But she'd pushed Jake too far before, even if only in jest; and had worn the marks on her arm to prove it for nearly a week.

"You make it sound like I'm lifting my skirts out there, not singing a tune or two." She handed back the hand-rolled cigarette with a grudging nod of thanks.

Jake stared at her with his usual hungry, calculating look. Between running this roadhouse, and running bootleg booze to Omaha and back, he was nothing if not a shrewd businessman. Or a mobster, depending on who was telling the tale.

"You could, you know. Lift your skirts, I mean. Just remember: I get my cut if you pick up johns inside the joint."

"No thanks." Clara hadn't been against trading a small favor or two for a ride home when this place shut down at three, but it wasn't something she did on the regular. Because more than anyone else, Clara Doyle relied on herself.

Besides, if she got into some guy's roadster in the parking lot, well, that was fair game. Her choices, her consequences. And she considered herself smart enough to not get caught, in more ways than one.

"At least I don't have to worry about you taking advantage of me, Jake," she said sweetly. "I've heard the rumors, like everyone else. It's no wonder you want to get those 'boys' out there riled up. Makes it easier for you, huh?"

As the manager shouted random insults in her direction, Clara started toward her dressing room. The back of the roadhouse was nearly as dark as the night outside, lit by only a bare bulb here and there. Jake was always looking to save a buck or two, including on the electric bill; and the gloom helped conceal the tarp-draped crates packed with bottles of illegal booze. The best hooch, of course, was kept in a locked storage room in the far corner of the joint.

The place reeked from the musty odor of the river flowing just a few yards from the back door, sweat, spilled booze, and who knew what else. As she rounded another corner in the maze, the heels of Clara's T-strap Mary Janes barely skirted a small puddle of something especially pungent.

The Swamp Stomp's past life had been as a warehouse for the brick factory that still operated across the dirt road. It was a silly name for a club, Clara had told Jake, even though it was in the river bottoms; it sounded more like a dance move. He'd challenged her to come up with something better, but she hadn't.

It didn't matter, anyway. When Prohibition arrived last year, and the fancy sign out front came down and the club shimmied over to the wrong side of the law, everyone began calling it Jake's Joint.

Her dressing room door was sticking more than usual tonight, thanks to the late-summer humidity, and it took all of Clara's not-considerable weight shoved against it to get it open.

Like so many other things at this club, the reality of this space was nowhere near as nice as its label. It wasn't much more than a closet, with another bare bulb dangling from its ceiling. A cracked secondhand mirror had been tacked over a scratched table, and a stool with not-quite-level legs shoved underneath it.

Clara reached for her tin of face powder, and swore. Its volume was noticeably lower than an hour ago, which meant that at least a few of the waitresses had helped themselves to its contents.

Because not only was this "dressing room" a dump, it was far from private. Especially since some of the other girls were eager to take Jake up on his skirt-raising offer for an extra buck or two. Clara had nearly died of mortification after her first gig (how had that been three years ago already?) when she'd stumbled in on one of those transactions taking place on this table.

But nothing shocked her anymore. Not the hookups happening in the shadows, inside the club or out; or the nose-clearing fumes from the "liquor" served at the club's bar. Rats scurried inside through the building's cracks when a storm was brewing, and whenever the river threatened to yet-again overflow its banks.

Unlike that small, low-key "restaurant" not far from Clara's home on the east edge of Eagle River, no one came here for the food. None was served, first of all; although patrons were allowed to cart in whatever they fancied.

People came here to get drunk and high. To forget about the distant spouse at home, the bills they couldn't pay, the Great War that had destroyed so many lives. They weren't really here for the music; it was just background noise for their hell-bent self-destruction.

But Clara was. In her life, music was just about the only thing that mattered.

She took one of the tattered washcloths off a nearby shelf, sniffed it and the water in the enamel basin to make sure both were relatively clean, and scrubbed the sweat and clumped powder off her face. If she was careful, the kohl already rimming her eyes would last the rest of the night. Her lipstick would have to be reapplied before she went back on stage, but Clara didn't care; she really, really, needed a drink.

Clara Doyle was the hot girl singer for the house band. On Friday and Saturday nights, and two rotating nights during the week, her impressive mezzo-soprano voice reached for the rafters on slow ballads and sank down deep for the jazz-blues tunes that set this place on fire. Her figure was curvy enough for most of the men, but still svelte enough for her to slip into the narrow-cut dresses that were all the rage.

She was "a doll that could really go places," according to that one promoter who'd breezed through here last month. Clara still suspected Chuck had become lost, then hopped off the train at the wrong stop in a substance-fueled haze. Why else would someone like him spend even five minutes in a backwater place like Eagle River?

Clara sighed as she ran her fingers through her waves again, tried to smooth them despite the stifling heat. She'd given Chuck too much of her time, along with other things, but he'd yet to write her even one line. She wouldn't make that mistake again.

She stared at herself in the mirror. Did her eyes always look this dead, this vacant, when she was this sober?

For one moment, she saw Abigail Doyle, the shy, skinny

girl who had impressed Miss Chaplan, Eagle River's lone music teacher, the first time Abigail belted out a song in class. Abigail would have loved to sing in a church choir (take your pick, there were three in this town) but the Doyles "didn't go for churchin'," according to her ham-fisted father.

Abigail had been lucky to make it through eighth grade, given that Ma had little Charlie the year before that. And Charlie hadn't been the last. Six babies in fifteen years; six that had survived, anyway. Ma had fought hard for Abigail, who was the oldest, to get at least a basic education before she was told to stay home and help raise the others. High school had never even been a discussion.

Abigail was also supposed to find herself a nice boy (meaning one that could provide, "nice" wasn't really a priority), preferably by the time she turned eighteen, and be one less hungry mouth at the table.

But too many of the boys who went off to the Great War didn't come home. A significant number of the ones who did had nerve damage from the mustard gas. All of them wept when they were drunk as they talked about Lys or the Somme, and foxholes, and friends cut down by machine guns.

Abigail had been desperate to find a way out of the family's crowded bungalow, which still didn't have an indoor bathroom (Pa hadn't gotten around to that yet) if only for a few nights a week.

When Jake decided to turn this old warehouse into a roadhouse in the spring of 1918, Abigail had been first in line to audition as the singer for the band.

Two weeks later she was Clara Doyle, slipping out after supper in an old dress she'd jazzed up with some discount sequins from Eagle River's lone millinery shop.

Boots were usually needed to walk the mile south to the club; the winding "road" wasn't much more than a mud-streaked path and she also had to cross the railroad tracks just west of the trestle. Clara carried her dancing shoes in a burlap bag, and brought home her wages and tips in a much-smaller pouch tucked inside her camisole.

But two weeks from tonight, sooner if she could manage it, her name, and her life, were going to change again. Clara Doyle was going to board a train, and step off in Chicago as Clara Randolph.

She'd been saving her money, except for what she handed Pa and Ma every week in exchange for them looking the other way regarding her choice of career. Pa had upped their cut last year when Clara announced she was going to bob her hair. In return, he'd dropped his threats to send her to an asylum.

There was enough for the train ticket, and her portion of three months' rent on the two-room flat a distant cousin shared with some other girls not far from Chicago's theater district. One of them was getting married, which meant the pull-out sofa in the matchbox-sized main room was up for grabs. There was also a bit of shelf space in the icebox, and a shared bathroom down the hall. To Clara, the place sounded crowded and chaotic and wonderful.

"Clara Randolph," she whispered as she stared at her cracked reflection. She smiled into the mirror, and was struck by the jaded expression her face naturally settled into these days.

She tried again. There, much better: hopeful, talented, and smart.

Clara wasn't really interested in acting, but it was going to be her best bet to get noticed for her singing.

She was no fool; along with money for the train ticket and the rent, she'd saved enough cash for food, a new wardrobe, and some other things to get herself settled.

Many nights she'd reached for the small notebook kept under the bed she shared with Lizzie, and ran the numbers over and over again, made sure they added up to the future she wanted. The orderliness of the transactions soothed her nerves, helped block out the shouts of rage echoing from her parents' room across the hall.

Clara Doyle had a plan. Clara Randolph was going to make sure it was followed to the penny.

So, why hadn't she left yet?

According to Clara's careful calculations, there'd been enough money in early July. She'd put it off, reasoned that a few more weeks at the club (summer was always the roadhouse's busiest season) would let her rake in more cash to make her move.

She'd been right, of course. But two days ago, there'd been a letter saying one of the other girls had a friend looking for a place to stay. Clara needed to stake her claim to the couch, and soon.

The weather would start to change in a few weeks, anyway, she reminded herself as she powdered her cheeks. Fall was a time to start over, start fresh, like back when she'd been in school. If she was going to go, she needed to do it now.

She was scared; she could admit it. Eagle River, as claustrophobic as it was, was all she'd ever known. Pa was difficult to manage, and Ma was almost as bad; but Clara was going to miss them, in a strange way.

And she was going to miss this place. This dirty, raucous roadhouse. Clara was its star, for what that was worth. The band guys were fun, and more talented than some might think. Even the waitresses, who were too often catty and sometimes cruel, had become like feuding sisters to Clara.

But she couldn't stay. She was almost twenty-three; even one more year here, at this joint and in this town, and Clara would be finished. She would be too old to be the "girl singer," and too jaded and too rough around the edges to be any marginally respectful man's wife.

The future stretched out ahead of her, but it was too overwhelming to contemplate all at once. All she saw, in her mind, were the gleaming train tracks that would take her away from here.

The eastbound coach left at a quarter after three on Monday, Wednesday, and Friday afternoons. There was always room in the passenger cars, Clara knew, because she'd scouted them out as they lingered for a short time in Eagle River before pulling away again.

She'd pack right after lunch, while Ma was down for her nap with the youngest two and Pa was still working at the mill. The ticket would have to be purchased at the very-last minute because, even dressed in respectable traveling clothes rather than satin and sequins, Clara was known in this town. But by the time anyone realized she was gone, it would be too late.

"Hey!" a female voice shouted, then a fist banged on the door. "Get outta there, it's my turn!"

Clara picked up her headband. Before she could even pin it in place, Rita barged her way in.

"Move over," Rita slurred as she shoved Clara aside. "I've got a date in ten, need to freshen up."

It wasn't exactly a date; and Rita seemed too strung out to even know what night this was, but Clara said nothing. It wouldn't do any good.

There was a bit more air to be had in the main room, even if it was full of smoke and tinged with an earthy smell that rushed in through the open doors and windows. Saturday nights were always busy, but the place was packed beyond capacity.

Clara had to admit, this was the perfect spot for a gin joint. While the brick factory across the road was still very much in business, it had scaled back some as more modern construction methods came into favor.

Given its age and condition, this former warehouse was too close to the river to serve as reliable storage these days, even for bricks. The company's current owners had been eager to sell it to Jake, especially since they received a cut of the roadhouse's profits along with their initial windfall.

This joint was one of the few places around where the various classes of society rubbed elbows, everyone co-conspirators in their quest to have a good time.

The kiln workers were among the first customers during the workweek, arriving from across the road when their daytime shifts ended. As the sun lowered toward the horizon, they were joined by other laborers and farmers, their wives and girlfriends, and a sizeable selection of the region's business leaders as well.

The beamed ceiling was high, which made for great acoustics, and Jake kept the bar well stocked. But the cavernous public space was barely a notch more refined than the private areas in the back. Only the hand-carved walnut bar was truly grand; Jake had bought it cheap from a bankrupt saloon based on the promise he'd hire enough men to get it out the door.

Several patrons waved to Clara or gave her a wink, depending on their gender, but the bar was where she wanted to be.

"It's a hot one, huh?" Raymond handed her a paper napkin, which passed for table service in this club. He was the best of the band's two sax players, but often found himself behind the bar when the place was this busy. Raymond was handsome enough for the ladies, but laid-back enough to not get into fistfights with the men. By Jake's standards, that made Raymond as valuable as Clara herself.

Next came her usual gin fizz; Raymond knew what she liked. She held up the glass, then passed the sort-of clear liquid under her nose.

Jake received a new shipment last night, and this stuff smelled better than the last. Clara briefly wondered what was in it, exactly, but still took a big gulp.

Raymond had noticed her evaluation. "There's some real

carbonation in there," he proudly pointed out. "It's Saturday, you know. We're pulling out all the stops."

Jake had caught Eddie lifting booze from the storage room Wednesday night, and beat him up pretty good. That left the band without a trombone player, as well as a musical director, until next weekend.

Raymond gave one of the ladies at the bar a knowing smile, then turned back to Clara and tipped his chin toward the stage. It was just some wooden pallets nudged into a platform, but it was good enough.

"What are you thinking for our last set?" Raymond asked Clara. "Maybe we should throw in some deep Delta stuff."

"Why not? Let's do it up right."

It wasn't just the strong liquor that caught in Clara's throat. Raymond didn't know her plans; no one did, except that cousin in Chicago. She'd write to everyone once she was settled.

"We're here to give these people what they want," she reminded her bandmate, "which is a damn good time. Most of them will be suffering greatly when they stumble into their church pews tomorrow morning. Might as well make it worth their while."

A man's elbow, clad in a very expensive shirt, nudged Clara's arm. "How about you make tonight worth my while, and we'll call ourselves even?"

"Hey, Ozzie." She nudged him back. "How are things down at the bank?"

"Almost as wild as they are here. Or at least, I wish they were."

His dazzling smile appeared, and all of it focused on Clara. They'd been chums in school, and a bit more than that a few times since then. Oswald Baxter's family ran Eagle River's bank, as well as many other things in this town.

The two of them couldn't be more different. Maybe that's why they got along so well.

"Abbie, isn't it about time for you to ditch this joint?"

Ozzie's use of her old nickname warmed Clara to her toes. And then, she paused with her glass halfway to her lips.

Had she slipped up somehow, maybe when she'd had too many of Raymond's gin fizzes, and shared her plans with Ozzie? Clara didn't think so, but ...

"How about you give up the singing, get a real job?" Ozzie went on. "You're a talented singer, don't get me wrong; but the bank pays well. We could use another counter girl. I always said you were the smartest one in our class, me included."

Relieved, Clara rolled her eyes. "Your father is never going to let a girl from the wrong side of the tracks work at that bank."

"I'm taking over in another year or so. Before you know it, it won't be up to him."

Ozzie wasn't just handsome; he radiated confidence as well as wealth. Clara noticed two women within three feet who were already listening in, figuring out a way to put themselves in Ozzie's sights.

"The old man wants to work on his golf swing. If I'm lucky, he and Mother will decide to spend half the year in Florida." Ozzie shrugged. "There won't be much for me to do. I'll have plenty of time for fun, and still be able to get the job done."

Ozzie's grandfather had founded Eagle River and brought in the railroad, all before he'd started the bank. Adolphus had been gone for a few years now, but he'd set aside enough cash to send his favorite grandson to Princeton.

Of course, there was that scandal that had abruptly ended Ozzie's tenure after junior year. Clara hadn't been able to uncover the details, but a laughing Ozzie had once told her it involved "gin, gambling and girls." As far as she knew, he had yet to give up any of those hobbies.

He'd spent a year back home, helping at the bank when he

wasn't partying, while his father called in some favors to get him accepted at Northwestern in Chicago. With his business degree finally completed, he'd returned to Eagle River in May. Ozzie was back to stay, and Clara was about to leave.

There had been a few moments over the years when Clara had pondered a life with Ozzie, one of the above-board sort, and decided it would never work.

They were close, in so many ways; but she wasn't cut out to be a banker's wife.

It was just as well, she reminded herself while Ozzie prattled on about his new Pierce-Arrow roadster. He loved to possess shiny, pretty things ... until he grew tired of them. That was why she'd always put him off, afraid of gambling her heart away.

Even tonight, with her time in Eagle River ticking to its end, she was determined to not give in.

"I have no doubt you'll make a go of it at the bank." She held up her glass, and Ozzie raised his. "But we couldn't be more different, you and I."

"Says who?" Ozzie put on a mock pout. "And what's all this nonsense about you being from 'the wrong side of the tracks'? You live on the north side of the rails, the same as about half of this town. And this dump ... sorry Raymond," he said before turning back to Clara, "is on the south side."

Ozzie was drunk, and repeating an observation he'd made too many times before. Clara's old friend took it for granted she'd be here next Saturday night, and the one after that, to hear him share it all over again.

"I still think you should come work for us," he finally said. "Father's a pain in the ass, I know; but it's Grandma Lena who really runs things. She likes you; likes your smarts. If I put in a good word, she'll..."

Clara's outburst of laughter drew the attention of several revelers leaning on the bar.

"I just love that woman." Clara's words came out a bit

slurred; Raymond hadn't skimped on the gin. "She did as much for this town as the old man, if not more so. But she's what, nearly ninety? Your father is probably done taking direction from her. Besides, respectable folks aren't going to come into the bank with a hussy like me at the counter."

"Reformed hussy." Ozzie leaned in close. "I'll make sure of that. In public, at least."

Another invitation. But Clara gathered her courage, and ignored it. Besides, there were a few other people she wanted to chat with tonight.

"Why don't you be a dear," she told Ozzie as she stepped back from the bar, "and have Raymond pour me another when he gets a chance?"

Clara's glass was nearly empty again by the time Raymond pointed at the clock. She gulped the rest of her drink, waved to her friends, and started for the back of the club.

They aren't really my friends, she reminded herself as she hurried away. *Everyone likes to say they know someone in showbiz.*

She shoved the dressing room door open again. *And this isn't anything more than a dark hole in a seedy riverbank bar. I'm getting out of here, and I'm not coming back.*

Someone pounded on the door just as Clara finished touching up her lipstick. This time, it was Jake.

"Five minutes!" he barked. "Bring the swing, girl! They're waiting for you."

Clara found her way down the dark hallway by heart, then heard the piano and trumpet blast out their first notes of the last set of the night.

Her final set here ... forever.

The joint erupted in cheers and shouts when she pushed through the faded curtains and put on a wide smile. Ozzie was down in front, hanging with two other guys in expensive suits and a too-young girl already on his arm.

"How are we doing tonight?" Clara asked the room. It was smoky, and stiflingly hot and damp, and far-too crowded. But to her, it felt like home.

There were more whoops and whistles as she briefly turned toward the band, both to give them an acknowledging lift of her hand and herself a chance to blink back those damn tears.

"Let's give them a few more for the road, boys!"

Clara stomped her heel on the splintered boards, tossed her hands toward the water-stained ceiling, and started to sing.

Egg Money

✻ 1933 ✻

"The chickens are out again!" Mama reported as she stared out the window above the kitchen sink.

She gave the water pump's handle one push, then another, and set the coffee pot on the range's back burner.

"Two of them are lounging on the sidewalk. Four others are running around in the garden plot. I saw two more in the weeds behind the pump house."

Gladys Kleiner counted as she wiped her hands on her apron.

"Well, that's eight of them, at least. I hate to think what the rest of them are up to. Those poor birds! Since their house was nearly blown off its foundation, they probably hardly know which way is north, and which is south."

A spring storm had ripped through Union township only days ago, and turned the chickens' aged coop into not much more than a leaning pile of loose boards. The sixteen members of the Kleiners' flock were bunking in the barn until the family could figure out what to do next.

But that didn't mean the birds wanted to stay inside. Or even, much to everyone's chagrin, limit their foraging to the confines of the spacious pasture.

"They must have found another hole in the fence last night," Gladys told her mother as she flipped fresh eggs in the skillet. "Maybe Elmer will be able to find it, and fix it, before sundown."

It was only the first week of May, but the post-dawn sky was empty of clouds and had nothing to offer but the promise of another hot afternoon. Elmer was already in the field with their draft horses, Bessie and Ben, preparing the soil to plant corn yet this week.

Thank goodness nothing was in the ground yet, either in the fields or in the garden, as the storm had brought hail large enough to strip leaves off tender stalks of vegetation. Other than the now-slanting chicken coop, the only damage at the Kleiner farm had been a few downed tree limbs.

Just like her daily hunt to uncover the chicken's fresh eggs in their makeshift quarters, Gladys was gathering all the blessings she could find and tucking them away for safekeeping. Her family was going to need every single one of them to get through this year.

They would plant fewer crops this time around, Gladys and Elmer had decided a few nights ago at the kitchen table, as the kerosene lantern shed light on last year's ledgers. Louise and Tommy had already gone to bed and Matilda, Gladys' mother, was reading her Bible in her room.

Crop prices were down, and the economic storm of the past several years seemed far from over. It was better to keep their seed costs and bets on the weather as small as possible, Elmer and Gladys had agreed, rather than risk running into more trouble and losing everything they had left.

"I could go out and see what's what," Matilda offered as she set the table. "Get them back in the pasture for a while, at least." Then she chuckled. "We could time them. See how long it takes them to execute their next jail break."

Gladys was weary, but she managed a smile. Mama had moved in after Papa died two years ago, and Matilda was always looking for ways to contribute, to help out. But she was sixty-four, and not as agile as she used to be.

Gladys didn't want Mama to fall, of course; but there was also the reality that if she did, and they needed to fetch Doctor MacLeod, money was as scarce as hens' teeth. The doctor was gracious about taking what people had to trade, but the Kleiners didn't have much to give away these days, either.

"Don't worry about the chickens." Gladys slid slices of bread into the range to make toast. "I need to go out after breakfast, and I'll round them up then. Why don't you see what's keeping the children? They'll be late for school if they don't hurry."

As Matilda turned down the front hallway and started up the stairs, Gladys went to the kitchen's back entrance, where a welcome breeze was coming through the screen door, and peered out past the porch. Sure enough, some of the hens were feasting on whatever insects they were plucking out of the weeds by the pump house.

Just like people, chickens were creatures of habit. Even though their house was askew, and they'd been transferred to the other side of the farmyard, the birds were determined to forage in their favorite places. Maybe it was just as well; they knew where the best snacks were hiding, and the more they dined on bugs, worms, and natural vegetation, the less supplemental feed they'd need to stay strong and healthy.

Their eggs (and the birds themselves, when they became too old to be producers) were an important source of protein for this family. Every vegetable scrap that couldn't possibly be eaten by the human residents of this farm was set aside for the chickens.

"We have to do something about that coop, and quick." Gladys shook her head as she turned back to pull the toast from the range before the slices burned. "Those girls have made it clear where they want to be."

Once the children had started their half-mile walk to school, and Matilda was washing the dishes, Gladys removed her kitchen apron and reached for the one she wore during outside chores. Both garments were faded and worn, but her farmyard apron was nearly threadbare in places.

If she searched through the rag bags, where the family's clothes and other fabric items landed after every bit of usual use had been wrung out of them, maybe she could find what she needed to patch this chore apron one more time. After all, it would be a far bigger challenge to maintain this dress if it was no longer properly protected.

As she started across the yard, the kitchen-scrap bucket in one hand and a straw hat on her head, Gladys reminded herself that her troubles were small compared to the ones so many faced these days.

The storm had dropped a tornado about two miles to the south and east, and the Hackett family had lost their home. Elias was planning to ride the rails to California in search of work in the citrus groves, while Frannie and their four children hoped to move in with relatives. Even so, Frannie had told Gladys, taking in five mouths to feed was too much to ask any one family to bear.

Frannie hoped to keep the two youngest children living with her, at least; the two oldest, both boys, would have to leave school and find some sort of employment. Fred, who was fifteen, was determined to follow his father West; Frannie was terrified for him.

The Hackett family was about to scatter to the winds; unfortunately, others were having to do the same. Which made Gladys feel even more guilty when, while rubbing clothes on the washboard or sweeping the dirt off the back porch, her thoughts turned to possible ways to escape.

Where might her family go where they could be free from this drought, of the hard times that never seemed to end?

But sometimes, when things were especially hard, Gladys thought of only herself for a moment, or five. What would it be like to pack an empty feed sack with a few changes of clothes, take some silver dollars from the glass jar buried in the dirt of the cellar, and start off down the lane before sunrise?

It was only one mile into Eagle River, to the depot. But a train ticket cost money. If Gladys walked south rather than west, she would meet up with the tracks where they angled toward town. She could wait in the weeds for a train not up to speed, latch on to whatever she could find, and toss her pack through an open freight car door.

More and more these days, Gladys found herself thinking about Abbie Doyle, a girl she'd known in school. Abbie had done that very thing, over a decade ago: Saved her money from singing at the roadhouse, bought a ticket for Chicago, and never looked back. Last Gladys had heard, Abbie was performing in swanky clubs and rubbing elbows with important people. There'd even been whispers that she'd gotten engaged to some uptown fellow with a mansion on Lake Shore Drive.

But Gladys wasn't going anywhere. Outside of an occasional flight of fancy, she didn't want to, anyway. Besides, as a woman traveling alone, she'd be in danger the minute she crawled into a train car.

There had been stories in the newspapers, items she and Elmer cut out before letting the children read the latest edition. Violence in all its ugly forms, against men as well as women and children. Like Gladys' old chore apron, this country was coming apart at the seams.

Even with her straw hat firmly in place, Gladys took advantage of the yard's shade trees as she made her way to the barn.

"Birdy-birds!" she shouted, and rattled the scrap bucket. "Get your grub before the others take it all!"

A buff-colored hen waddled out from behind the pump house, then two more clucked their way over from where they'd been hunting bugs along the lane.

By the time Gladys reached the barn's main door, she had twelve hens crowded around her dusty boots. That meant four more were still at large, including Flossie.

That crazy bird was one of Gladys' favorites, but the hen didn't like to play by the rules. Maybe that was why Gladys liked her so much.

Gladys took a moment to enjoy the comparatively cool air inside the barn. The musty, comforting smell of straw and hay still filled this space, even if the hayloft's stacks were becoming terribly low for this early in the year.

Clover, the family's only cow, mooed a greeting and twitched her soft ears as the hens clucked and squawked their way down the aisle.

"I know, I know." Gladys rubbed Clover's forehead as she checked the cow's water bucket. Elmer had filled it before he took the horses out to the fields. "They make for noisy neighbors, don't they? I wish I knew how long they were going to stay. Maybe you should head out into the pasture for a stroll before it gets too hot."

Just a few years ago, this barn had been full of life. A lump formed in Gladys' throat as she gazed at the vacant spaces down the way and across the aisle.

Along with Pansy, the other milk cow, the Kleiners' five beef cattle had been sold last year to pay off debts. All the pigs had gone, too; although Elmer hoped to barter for a young one from a neighbor soon. Clover's only roommates these days were a couple of barn cats that came and went; and now, these displaced chickens.

"Here you go." Gladys filled two of the chickens' dented metal pans with kitchen scraps, and the others with scoops of feed from a sealed bucket kept in a vacant stall across the way. By the time she returned with more water from the pump house, Flossie had found her way into the barn.

"This is what happens when you stick to your own schedule," Gladys scolded the bird, who pushed her way in wherever she thought the best snacks were hiding. "What's left is what you get."

Gladys and Matilda were going to bake this morning, before it got too hot. She needed to get to the house, but Gladys decided to take the long way around to the back porch. She wanted to finalize this year's garden plan while her hands were busy with the bread dough.

Bessie and Ben would turn the garden's soil as soon as the crops were planted, and then it would be time to rehome the seedlings that had been started indoors. Unlike the Kleiners' plans for their cash crops, the garden needed to be as large and diversified as possible. It had to keep their bellies full all growing season, then provide enough vegetables to preserve in August to sustain them through the winter.

Perhaps the tomatoes should move to the southwest corner? Gladys studied the still-vacant patch of ground with an experienced eye. Maybe pumpkins on the east side, this time. Green beans and peppers here, several rows of sweet corn there, then potatoes and carrots and turnips ...

Gladys hated turnips. But they grew like weeds and were reliable producers. Some varieties made for good animal feed, as well; she had to find a spot for them.

There would be long hours spent in the hot sun, weeding and watering and harvesting; but if she managed the garden right, her family would have enough to eat. They could ration kerosene and use more candles, cut wood from their own trees when the price of coal was too high. Gladys and Matilda could turn everyone's clothes inside out and make them last longer.

Every single day, Gladys was grateful that the Kleiners owned their home.

Papa had given Gladys and Elmer this land as a wedding present. They'd lived in its original, much-smaller home for two years until the current house was built. The couple had chosen this foursquare Craftsman design from a catalog, and most of the materials were shipped to Eagle River by train. One branch of the Kleiner family had operated Eagle River's brick kiln for well over fifty years, and Elmer's parents had offered discounted building supplies as their own after-the-fact wedding gift.

The two-story house was spacious and welcoming, with a wide front porch that faced west toward town. It was only nine years old and sometimes, Gladys still couldn't believe she lived somewhere so fine. She and Elmer had planned to fill it with children, but a large family was a dream Gladys was certain would never be realized.

Farming had never been easy, and the dark times that arrived after the crash of '29 had made Gladys and Elmer lower those expectations. Louisa was now ten, Tommy was seven; they'd agreed to stop there. They simply couldn't afford more children. Especially after Mama had moved in.

It was a constant source of worry, month in and month out. Elmer and Gladys kept a careful eye on the calendar, of course; but that wasn't reliable enough. Doc MacLeod refused to discuss other options, even with his married patients, but certain prevention items were sold under the guise of "feminine hygiene" in the backs of the newspapers and magazines. It meant parting with some of their closely guarded money, but Elmer and Gladys had agreed the items were a necessity.

If only there was some way to get more cash, Gladys mused as she looked around the farmyard. That was what this family desperately needed.

In the bright morning sunshine, the battered chicken coop was as forlorn as ever. One of the doors still miraculously clung to its tilted frame; the other had been found thirty feet away, bashed against the pasture fence. The family had gathered every scrap of loose lumber and stacked it in the pump house. The coop's windows, of course, had been shattered.

Gladys had left the main barn door open, as it was obvious the chickens were determined to forage where they pleased. Maybe it was just as well; if any of the hens dropped an egg while roaming the pasture, Clover might smash it with a hoof before it was found.

With their home destroyed, the chickens were making perches wherever they could find them. Two had just tucked themselves into the lowest branches of the young maple tree on the side of the garden. They looked rather ridiculous, scooched in there like that. Gladys told them so, even as she admired how these birds snatched up every opportunity available to them.

When she turned back toward the damaged coop, Gladys suddenly saw so much more than what was visible. She examined it closely for a few minutes, and her ideas for the garden were temporarily pushed aside.

Those crafty, crazy chickens ... they were the answer.

Elmer waved as he and the team came closer to the farmyard, and Gladys returned her husband's greeting with more enthusiasm than she'd had just moments ago.

He'd take a short break right after lunch. Between now and then, Gladys was going to come up with a plan.

* * *

"I think we should expand the flock," Gladys told her husband as they stared at what was left of the chicken coop.

"If we get more chickens, there will be more eggs. And more meat later on, too. Maybe we can find some chicks locally. Or there's always the hatchery."

The more this flock could produce, the more opportunities the Kleiners would have to sell whatever they could spare. Not everyone in town had their own chickens, and some of the rural residents had given up their flocks in the past few years. Everyone was cutting back, looking to take on less risk; the Kleiners had been doing the same.

But this ... this was one time Gladys was certain they needed to do the opposite.

Even so, more chicks to raise meant more money upfront: extra feed, additional shelter, more room to roam. It was a gamble, with things as tight as they were these days, but Gladys was ready to take that risk. Was her husband?

Elmer was her partner in life, they were a team. Even so, she knew this was going to be a hard sell.

He seemed surprised by her ideas, yet intrigued. "We could sell eggs at the mercantiles, once we had a reliable surplus," he said slowly as he rubbed the stubble on his chin. "And at the creameries, too."

"That's what I was thinking. But we'll need to make the coop bigger, this time around. An addition, if you will, for the new birds to have enough space. We could put the extra nesting boxes in there, too."

Elmer thought Bessie and Ben might be able to pull the coop back to something sort-of square. There was extra scrap lumber piled in a few corners of the barn; these days, nothing was ever thrown away.

"The biggest issue would be the windows," he said. "We'll have to buy those."

"Screens will do until fall; I think there is some wire mesh left on that roll. But, yes; we'll have to put aside some money for windows before winter."

What Gladys really wanted, what this flock would need as it expanded, was a whole new chicken house.

She could see it, in her mind: Three times this size, with plenty of windows for ventilation and light. Greater height in the middle so it was easier to collect the eggs and feed the hens. A steeper, taller roof on the back half that allowed for another row of windows just under the pitch. She'd need a ladder to reach those, but it would be worth it.

Gladys was determined to have the very-best chicken coop not only in Union Township, but throughout Hartland

County. But today wasn't the time to share her full dream with her husband. They just needed to make a start. Find the courage, and a bit of cash, to take these first steps. Someday, when things were better, they could build the chicken house she envisioned.

Elmer stepped to the west side of the coop's foundation, and held out his hands. "I think we can add on here. Even three-by-four feet would help. If we don't have enough building supplies, I might be able to barter for them." Then he laughed. "You know what else we might need someday? A rooster."

Gladys was so relieved. She threw her arms around her husband, and buried her face in his worn shirt.

"Whatever it takes, so that you never have to leave us. I never want you to have to go to California. I want our family to stay together, always."

"I'm not going anywhere." He kissed the top of her hair, then kissed her properly. Then he smiled. "Except back out to the field."

Elmer was about to turn away, then stopped and placed one hand on his wife's cheek. "You are a wonder, Gladys Kleiner. We are going to get through this."

* * *

The aroma of fresh-baked loaves cooling on the counter filled the house that afternoon. Gladys and her mother carefully laid out items for mending on the dining-room table, and worked their way through the overalls, dresses, and shirts.

As she reinforced buttons and tacked on patches, Gladys' mind flew as fast as her nimble fingers. Her ideas for expanding the flock, and Elmer's enthusiasm for the project, had her looking to the future with more hope than she'd felt in several months.

When the children came home from school, Tommy went

out to clean the occupied areas of the barn and Louisa picked up her own needle.

"I'm running out of good denim pieces for these overalls," Gladys said to Louisa not half an hour later. "Why don't you come upstairs with me, and we'll see what we can find in the bottom of the other scrap bag?"

But there was so much more to this errand. With all the possibilities the day had brought, it seemed like the perfect time to share a secret with Louisa.

Gladys reached into the back of her and Elmer's closet and pulled out the second scrap bag. Louisa joined her on the edge of the bed, and they began to sort through the contents.

"This might work for Papa's overalls." Louisa held up a leftover denim leg. "Is there enough so all the patches can match?"

"I think so. What a good find! Reach back down in there, all the way to the bottom. See if you find anything else."

Louisa frowned in confusion, then pulled out a small denim pouch tied closed with a length of red string. "What's this? It's heavy."

Gladys took the small bag, and loosened its strings. "I wanted to show this to you. You're old enough to know about this; but don't tell your brother."

Louisa nodded solemnly. At ten, she was honored to be let in on an adult-world secret. Then she gasped as a pile of coins glinted in the afternoon light.

"It's money! Mama, where did you get this?"

"From the chickens." Gladys couldn't keep the pride out of her voice. "On many farms, ours included, the chickens are mostly women's work. You know we sell eggs from time to time. This is where I keep the proceeds."

She settled the pouch back in her astonished daughter's hands. "It's egg money, Louisa. Our egg money buys school supplies for you and Tommy, shoes for all of us, and so many other things we can't barter or trade for. Papa and I have decided to expand our flock, to make more money if we can. We will all have to pitch in to make this a success." She pointed at the humble sack. "And this is why that is so very important."

Louisa stared at the pile of money. "I knew about the jar in the cellar. But not this."

"And that's still where most of what we have is kept, especially since the banks are struggling these days. That money, as you know, is for taxes and other big expenses."

Gladys reached into the pouch, and held up a quarter. "But this money? It's different. Oh, these days, every penny is dear. But someday, when things are better, this money can also be for extras, little things here and there."

She carefully retied the little purse, and settled it back in the bottom of the scrap bag. And then, she took her daughter's hands in her own.

"The egg money itself is important, of course, but it's more than just nickels and silver dollars. I want to tell you something Grandmama told me, when I was about your age. Someday you'll marry, and you'll need to understand this." Gladys grinned. "Who knows, maybe it'll be one of the Trowbridge boys from down the road?"

Was Louisa blushing, just a little? It was too early for some other discussions, thank goodness. But this one, today, seemed more relevant than ever.

"Farming is a hard life, even in good times," Gladys warned her daughter. "Everything and everyone must work together to make it successful. And usually, it's the husband who handles the accounts, pays the bills. But egg money? That's the wife's to do with as she sees fit. Does that make sense?"

Louisa thought it over, then nodded. "Something that's all mine." The eagerness in her voice filled Gladys with pride. She was raising this girl right, if Louisa saw the value of finding a little independence along the way.

"Like a new hat! Or, if we're short some month, I can reach into my stash and say, 'here's what we need, right here!'"

There was power in money, a sense of equality. Gladys knew that; Louisa was learning it, too. And if Gladys ever had another daughter, she would share this same lesson with her.

But never mind that now. Louisa's eyes had been opened to the possibilities nestled inside a little bag tied with string; that was enough for today.

"Let's go downstairs." Gladys handed the denim pieces to her daughter, then tucked the scrap bag back inside the closet. "Maybe we can get those overalls finished before we have to start supper."

On the Shelf
✳ 1945 ✳

Irene felt rather sentimental as she thumbed through the Eagle River Public Library's ledger. How was it December again? Christmas was only a few days away, and 1946 waited just beyond that.

She added the overdue-book fines that had been collected this week to December's revenue tally, then moved on to the rest of the facility's accounts.

Both the bank and the ladies' aid society had offered donations recently. The library could always use more books, of course; Irene would earmark most of the bank's funds for those. Perhaps a few new magazine and newspaper subscriptions? Television was the future, everyone said so; but Eagle River's library director couldn't fathom a day when that new medium would replace the periodicals she kept neatly arranged in the main reading area.

The Eagle River Ladies' Aid Society had been especially generous, given that it had resumed its original focus on veterans and their families. The same had occurred during the first World War, Irene had heard, even as the club continued to raise money for other charitable needs in the community.

A few more right-sized chairs could be added to the children's area, Irene decided.

Or maybe, she should purchase a thick rug so the library's youngest patrons could comfortably gather on the floor during story time. Eagle River's Carnegie library was grand and beautiful, with spacious windows and ornate woodwork, but the oak floors were hard regardless of how much they shined.

Those purchasing decisions, however exciting they might be, wouldn't be finalized until after the holidays. Irene Miller double-checked her figures, then noted there was just enough room on this page for whatever else might yet be added in 1945.

Empty pages, full of possibility and promise, came next in the ledger. As the heavy, ivory paper gleamed in the light of Irene's desk lamp, she wondered what the new year might bring. The past several years had been difficult for everyone, herself included; it was hard to work up too much hope, at least not yet. Even during this special season.

The war was finally over, yet everyone was still waiting for normal life to return. And so many of the men, as well.

Leo Shaw, Irene's boyfriend, was drafted in 1942. After basic training, he'd been granted a stateside office-duty post that was the answer to Irene's prayers. But as the conflict deepened, Leo shipped out to the Pacific Theatre.

His letters became less frequent, and more of their lines were snipped out by the censorship office.

Irene soon considered herself lucky to get a short note every few months that told her what Leo's platoon had to eat (nothing good) and how often he missed her (every hour of every day).

Leo wouldn't be home for the holidays, but he was expected back in Eagle River just a few weeks later. They planned to marry, of course, and farm with his parents east of town. Irene was already twenty-eight, and Leo was a year older. There was so much to plan, so much to do, before the next part of both their lives could begin.

Leo had been away for almost four years. Had he changed?

Other than some old photos, all Irene had of Leo these days, all she'd had for far too long, were his letters; and they didn't tell her much.

Of course he's changed, she reminded herself for what had to be the hundredth time. It would be impossible for him not to, after what he'd been through. *Besides, I've changed, too.*

There was another letter, not from Leo, that weighed on Irene's mind these days. It waited in the wooden keepsake box, the one that also held all his letters, under her bed at the boarding house. Some nights, as Irene tossed and turned, grappled with what sort of decision she might make, that lone envelope might as well have been a rock jammed into her mattress.

Irene pushed those jumbled thoughts away, then rolled her chair toward the office window overlooking Main Street. It was only three-thirty in the afternoon, but the skies were darkening with the promise of more snow.

Red-and-green decorations danced on the ornate lamp posts. Garlands were draped over many of the businesses' front doors, and their windows were filled with gifts for all ages and budgets. Residents bustled about, fedoras held tight and purses clutched close against the rising wind.

While a few cars and trucks were parked along Main Street, Irene knew most of the shoppers who lived in town were on foot. Gasoline, among so many other things, had been heavily rationed for so long. Those restrictions had finally been lifted, but there were still some shortages.

Irene had managed to score a heavily used bicycle a few years ago, but it was useless in this kind of weather. Her family farmed west of town, between Eagle River and Prosper, and her father was going to fetch her for the few days over Christmas when the library would be closed.

Irene needed a distraction; preferably a positive one. Since no more would be found in the ledger this afternoon, she turned to the latest edition of her favorite literary journal. Maybe she could start a list of likely titles to add to the shelves.

She'd barely made it through the biography section when she heard a commotion out by the circulation desk.

A man's excited voice echoed down the hall. Then Marjorie said, "why yes, Mr. Freitag, she's in the back."

Irene patted her dark waves and adjusted her cardigan as heavy footsteps hurried in her direction. In a matter of seconds, the president of the library board burst into her office.

Edmund Freitag's glasses were still fogged over from the damp chill outside. The older man was in a rather agitated state, with his wool overcoat half-unbuttoned and his winter hat tilted at a dangerous angle. Irene wondered if something of note had occurred at the pharmacy, then decided Mr. Freitag had enjoyed a too-long lunch at Paul's Place.

The little bar and restaurant, which was on the east side of town, doubled as a quiet daytime hangout for Eagle River's business leaders. And even from four feet away, Irene could easily detect the whiskey on Edmund's breath.

But her eyes were quickly drawn to the scrap of paper he pulled from his pocket after he'd closed the office door. It looked like a telegram. Too often during recent years, those tiny notes had brought terrible news.

"Mr. Freitag." Irene sat taller in her director's chair and tried to remain calm, as he certainly wasn't. "What brings you in today?"

"My girl, I bring you glad tidings!" Edmund chuckled as he unwound his maroon scarf with his free hand. "I have the most wonderful news on this cheerful holiday afternoon! I was on my way back to the pharmacy, but I just had to stop in."

The store only closed for half an hour at midday, which told Irene that Mrs. Freitag had been running the place alone for three hours. Even so, Edmund helped himself to the chair on the other side of Irene's desk.

"Everyone's buzzing about it." He waved the white slip of paper as if it were some sort of flag.

"Walt's on his way home! He's being discharged from the hospital just after New Year's. Eagle River's most decorated war hero will be back before you know it. We'll need to plan a ceremony! But with all the cold and the snow, we can't have it in the park. And city hall is too formal, don't you think?"

He didn't wait for Irene to share an opinion. "I say, here at the library is the perfect place! After all, this is where Walt belongs."

Edmund's excitement blinded him to the shock Irene was certain showed on her face.

"Walt's made a miraculous recovery, and he plans to be back at work by February first." He slapped the telegram on Irene's desk. "You can tell he's an Eagle River chap, for sure. He's not going to let those crutches get him down!"

Walter Deegan was the library's director. Or he had been, until he'd been drafted early in 1943. Irene, who'd obtained her education certificate at the Iowa State Teachers College in Cedar Falls and was teaching elementary students in Prosper at the time, hadn't hesitated to apply for the library vacancy. All her life, books had been her friends. She'd been at the top of her college literature classes, and scored impressive mathematics marks, as well. The Eagle River library board had been eager to hire her for this position.

What Irene didn't have, however, was the library science degree Walter Deegan possessed. Nor did she have a wife and two children to support.

Walt had saved five members of his platoon during an ambush in western Germany earlier in the year. His injuries had put him in the hospital for months, and he was coming home with a barely usable right leg along with a medal for his bravery under fire.

Irene had nothing against Walt; like everyone else, she'd hoped he would return to Eagle River. But there had always been a glimmer of hope that he might want a fresh start after the war. Perhaps he'd leverage his education and charm into a different field, such as sales. He certainly had the sociable manner that career required.

Edmund was impatiently waiting for Irene to join in his merriment. She swallowed her disappointment, and gave a nod of understanding that she didn't quite feel.

"So you are here to fire me, Mr. Freitag. When will be my last day?"

"Oh, Irene!" Edmund shook his head sadly, as if she were a puppy that had messed on the rug. *So sensitive; you know how the ladies can be!*

"No one is firing you, my girl. You've done a wonderful job keeping our little boat afloat while Walt's been away. There's no reason to rush off; we'll need you here until he is ready to resume his duties. Besides, you and Leo will be getting married. Settling down, starting a family. You'll have more important things to do."

Irene wanted to remind the library board president that this "little boat" served residents from miles around Eagle River, in addition to everyone in town. There were book clubs for adults, story times for children, seasonal activities all year long. Two spacious rooms that were booked solid for club meetings and community gatherings.

Along with a fleet of volunteers, she had two part-time staffers to manage. Marjorie and Ralph helped her clean this library from top to bottom every week; and Irene maintained a shoestring budget where every purchase, every expense, was justified.

A budget that had been a haphazard mess when Irene took over the books two years ago. Littered with half-hearted summaries and incomplete ledger entries, it had taken Irene weeks to crack Walt's codes. This office had been just as cluttered, with stacks of books piled on every surface (including the floor!) and the unmistakable stench of pipe tobacco soaked into everything in the room.

From what Irene could gather, Walt had spent most of his time with his feet up on this desk, reading a newspaper; then had charmed his way through his monthly meetings with the board.

"Do you need me to turn in a formal resignation?" Irene was determined to keep her emotions in check. "Make it official?"

"Oh, let's not worry about that. This has been the plan all along, as you know. Everyone's expecting it."

Edmund did seem sorry, Irene decided. At the very least, he seemed sorry to be the one elected to share this news with her.

The pity on his face was painful to see. If he reached over the desk and tried to pat her on the head, which he almost seemed inclined to do, she was going to throw the ledger at him.

"I would think you'd be happy about this," Edmund said. "This has been so much hard work for you. For all of you ladies." He shook his head in awe. "You know, the girls who've gone off to the factories, kept the assembly lines going while the boys have been away. Worked in the shops, put in the crops. Of course, there's those who've joined up, in their own little way, and served all over the world. Just think of those nurses!"

That last idea seemed nearly impossible for Edmund to comprehend. He considered it for a moment, then moved on.

"It was the same for all of us, the last time around." Edmund had served in the First World War. "But it's time for us to get back on track. Not just here, but everywhere."

He leaned forward in his chair. "You must be tired, Irene.

All of you must be so very tired. It'll be such a relief to get back to your homes and families, I would think."

What Irene didn't say, what she wanted to scream at Edmund until his whiskey-flushed face turned a darker shade of red, was that running this library had been the highlight of her existence. Making decisions, balancing the books, working with her staff. Seeing how this institution bettered the lives of people for miles around had given Irene energy and purpose, a sense of accomplishment that not even teaching had provided.

Edmund also didn't seem to understand that "being at home" was an every-waking-moment sort of job. Far more hours in the day than he spent running his pharmacy.

Irene mustered a sense of calm she didn't really feel, and rose from her chair. Perhaps the board president would take the hint, and wander back to his business.

"I'll start preparing for Walter's return," she promised. "My staff will begin in earnest after the holidays, as we have our yearly inventory to complete in the coming week."

"Of course, of course." Edmund nodded vigorously. "And I really want to thank you for all that you did in Walt's absence. I'm sure the rest of the board feels the same. The whole town, come to think of it. Well, I'll be off. Merry Christmas!"

He wouldn't shake her hand; that would indicate she was his equal. It was just as well, as Irene needed both palms on the edge of the desk to steady herself.

"Merry Christmas." She managed a small smile before the board president hurried away.

Irene was surprised, although maybe she shouldn't be. Sad; and angry, too. Especially because, now that she thought about it, Mr. Freitag had just offered his appreciation in a way that hinted her work here was already done.

Walt wouldn't be back for six weeks; more, if he happened to encounter any delays. Too often, the wheels of the military's bureaucracy were slow to turn. And the ships and trains were overcrowded with soldiers making their way home, had been for months.

There was plenty of work to be done at this library in the meantime. Inventory needed to be completed by the end of the year; she needed to focus on the tasks at hand.

Irene flipped the literary journal closed, and tucked her barely started list inside its cover. What did it matter now? Walt would be the one to decide how to spend those donations, along with everything else.

"Is everything alright?" Marjorie eyed her boss with concern as Irene approached the circulation desk. "Mr. Freitag is certainly jolly this afternoon. A liquid lunch will do that to a man."

Irene had to laugh, despite her troubles. "He definitely has Santa beat in that department. Mr. Freitag was just checking in, since there isn't another board meeting until after the holidays."

She hated to keep such big news from Marjorie. But Irene needed some time to digest it, to figure out how to navigate the situation with the library's patrons as well as her staff.

Ralph, who was seventeen and a high-school senior, had narrowly missed the draft. Marjorie was nineteen, and a sharp judge of character. Irene had to wonder if that would work in her favor when Walt returned, or the opposite.

School had just let out for the day, and Ralph soon arrived. Irene gave him a few moments to remove his cap and coat before she waved him over to the circulation desk.

"Can you please watch the counter?" Irene asked him. "We are going to focus on inventory until close."

"Sure thing, Miss Miller."

Whenever someone called her that, Irene felt as if she were back in the classroom. Could she go back to teaching?

Irene considered that possibility as she and Marjorie headed for the "G-J" fiction stacks. She certainly was qualified, but there was one problem: It was still frowned upon for teachers to be married.

That was the biggest reason Irene and Leo had waited so long. She'd wanted to have a career for a while, and he'd wholeheartedly supported her.

No, Irene decided. Leo had waited long enough. So had she. Wasn't that what she wanted, more than anything? To start her new life with him?

A wooden crate, one-third full of old books, waited on a wheeled cart at the end of the row. Irene reached for the notepad and pencil she'd abandoned just before lunch, and focused on the task at hand.

The Eagle River library aimed to keep as many items in circulation as possible; but sometimes, titles needed to be tossed to make room for new books. While the bestsellers and classics were well known by library staff, so many other books drew less interest from the public. During their annual inventory counts, the employees culled unpopular books that were damaged.

"How about you take that top section?" Irene suggested to Marjorie, who had her own notebook and pencil. "Maybe we can get started on the 'H's yet today."

"It's rather sad, isn't it?" Marjorie sighed as she added three obvious discards to her pile. "They've been waiting and waiting for someone to choose them. For the chance to go on an adventure, see new places." She held up a faded leather tome whose cover was coming apart. "Or at least, for someone to make them whole again."

Yes, Irene decided. That was exactly how she felt, especially these days. Waiting, always waiting. Waiting for Leo to come home. Waiting to see what the future might hold, what her own fate would be.

She held out her hand, and Marjorie passed her the book in question. Irene shook her head; this one was definitely too far gone.

"I wish we could repair them all," she told Marjorie as she carefully set the book inside the crate. "We just don't have the budget, or the time."

This was such a difficult task, deciding which books had to go and which got to stay. For one more year, at least. Irene studied her own row, and found several more books that were just as Marjorie had described.

As Edmund Freitag had reminded her, several young women from Eagle River had taken the opportunity to see the world (or at least leave town) during the long years of this terrible war.

Irene had classmates and friends who'd decamped to Des Moines to work at an ordnance plant there. Others joined the women's units of the various armed forces. Their occasional letters had been filled with excitement over the places they'd been, the things they'd seen. The people (and often, the soldiers) they'd met.

Some of it had been dangerous work, Irene knew that. But it all sounded so glamorous. Away from their parents, husbands, and sweethearts, out of reach of the expectations put upon them by day-to-day life in a small town, those women had taken advantage of all the freedom they could find during such a horrible situation.

And Irene, what had she done? She'd stayed, of course. Like so many of the books on these shelves, Irene hadn't budged more than a few inches in the past four years. And her two acts of independence were about to end. Walt was taking back his job, and Irene would have to move in with her parents until she and Leo got hitched.

Had she done enough with the time she'd been given? Could she have done more?

Irene carefully considered two shabby novels on the next shelf, but decided to grant them pardons. Their section wasn't crowded, and the titles were more dusty than damaged.

She shouldn't be so hard on herself, Irene decided. She'd

done her duty, right here in her hometown. Perhaps she wasn't cut out for the kind of adventure some of the other young women craved.

As hard as it might be to adjust to what society expected of her now, Irene knew she was going to have a far easier time than some of her friends. A few had already declared they were never coming back to Eagle River. They'd changed too much, they'd written to Irene; it was too late.

And what about Leo? He'd been sent halfway around the world; then compelled to do, and see, unspeakable things. How was he going to settle down, pick up his old life here? How could she help him make the transition? Was she still sure, after all these years apart, that she even wanted to?

But as she evaluated another section of books, Irene had to face the fact that it didn't really matter. She had already been shrugging off the "spinster" label before the war began. She'd made her choice, many years ago; it was done.

The library stacks suddenly seemed so tall, too close together. There wasn't enough light, or air.

"Hey," Marjorie said behind her, then Irene heard the creak of the cart's wheels. "Here, sit on the edge for a moment. You're so pale."

"I'm fine." Irene managed a smile. "Perhaps I'm coming down with a cold."

"I'll get you some water."

"There's no need. But, thank you." She turned to look her assistant in the eye. "You've been such a great help to me. I hope you know what a difference you've made here."

"A difference?" Marjorie shrugged. "Oh, I don't know. But I've loved working here. Even when I was a little girl, I used to imagine myself doing this very thing."

There was a note of resignation in Marjorie's voice, one that was especially notable given that she was still so young. Then she leaned in, a weathered novel clutched in one hand.

"Carl and I are going to elope the second he gets back next

month." Marjorie's face was suddenly alight with excitement. "We can't wait to start our life together! I'm not going to give my notice yet, because it's still a secret. But I wanted you to know."

Marjorie's beau had only shipped out in June, and he was already on his way back from the war. They'd been apart for six months, which was an eternity for Marjorie but only a fraction of the time Irene and Leo had been separated.

"I'm so happy for you both!" Irene meant it. "We'd love to have you for as long as you'd like to stay."

Walt wasn't likely to keep Marjorie around if she were married; but it sounded like Carl was going to beat him home, anyway.

As they returned to their tasks, Irene had to acknowledge how different the two of them were. Marjorie's period of independence had been so short; she probably hadn't had a chance to really see it for what it was. Irene wondered if, someday, her younger friend would look back and feel differently about her choices.

* * *

Mrs. Webster served supper promptly at five-thirty, but there was just enough time for Irene to mail a package to her sister.

After checking that the library's front doors were secure, Irene lingered for a moment on the wide steps, staring up at the gracious, elegant building as the first snowflakes started to fall.

This library had been her home for almost three years. She'd come back as a patron, but it wouldn't be the same.

She adjusted her knit hat and scarf, buttoned her wool coat to the very top, and turned north. It was less than two blocks to Eagle River's main intersection, where the still-unfrozen river rushed under the Main Street bridge.

The crossing had been rebuilt twice since the town was

founded. The current bridge was a modern marvel, a feat of engineering crafted by the WPA during the Great Depression. Along with two lanes for traffic, it had a wide walking path along its east side.

The business district picked up again on the north side of the bridge, and it was barely more than a block to the post office. That cinder-block building was only ten years old, another WPA project, and its wide front windows gave it a modern air.

Inside, there was a line. As she stomped the snow off her boots and waited her turn, Irene studied the rows of photographs on the lobby's bulletin board.

Right after Pearl Harbor, Mr. Kemp moved the community notices to the wall next to the counter. He'd then transformed the bulletin board into a display honoring all the Eagle River residents serving in the war. The space had soon become crowded with rows of photographs shared by the soldiers' families and friends.

Sadly, it hadn't been long before the postmaster had to create a second, smaller section for those who would never return. Just a few months ago, he'd created a third.

Now, there were sections for "serving," "lost," and, finally, "home."

Irene stared at Leo's snapshot on the board, which was the same one she carried in her wallet. In a matter of weeks, his photo would move to the "home" section. Her hands were icy from her walk, and her face pinched by the cold wind. But Irene's heart, which had received quite a shock that afternoon, began to thaw as she waited in line.

"Well hello, Irene." Mr. Kemp reached for the tape measure he kept in one apron pocket, and checked the size of her parcel. "I'm sure you've heard the good news: Walter Deegan's coming home."

"Yes." She took a deep breath as two women behind her started whispering to each other. She might as well come up with a simple, positive response, one she could rely on over and over again in the coming days.

"Yes, I certainly have. The library employees are looking forward to his arrival."

Mr. Kemp gave her a sympathetic smile as she handed him her coins; he understood the way of things.

As Irene turned away, the two women watched her closely. There was no sympathy in their stares, she was sure of that. Judgement, perhaps. Maybe jealousy. They knew that Irene's job, which had given her a prominent role in this community, was about to disappear.

She refused to duck her head in defeat. Instead, she gave them a big smile before she started for the door.

That terrible war had given Irene an extraordinary opportunity. Yes, she was about to lose it; but she decided right then to never let remorse cloud her memories of her time as library director. She would always take pride in how she'd managed the building and the staff, gave people a comforting place to connect with each other during those dark years.

Irene's steps were lighter as she went back across the bridge and walked the last blocks to her boarding house.

It had once been a grand home; the house was still welcoming, with wide porches and intricate trim that needed a little paint. The house offered eight rooms for boarders, with common areas on the first floor. Only women lived there; most of them had come to Eagle River for work during the war.

When Irene opened the front door, she was welcomed by the chatter of some of the women gathered around the fireplace in the front parlor. If her nose was correct, roast beef was on the menu tonight. She pulled off her gloves, waved to the others, then went straight to the steps.

There would be time to visit later. But first, Irene needed to get out of her damp clothes. And take a few minutes to prepare herself for what was sure to be an onslaught of questions about Walter Deegan.

Her room was at the front of the house, with two windows that looked over the front lawn. The home had a coal-fired furnace, thank goodness; but Mrs. Webster still permitted the ladies to enjoy fires in their rooms' grand hearths when it was bitterly cold.

Irene shrugged out of her coat, pulled off her boots, and carefully set her purse in the threadbare reading chair by the unlit fireplace. She switched on the lamp next to the bed, then knelt to pull out the wooden box that waited underneath.

She reached into the nearly full box and pulled out two stacks of Leo's letters. Both piles were tied with blue ribbon; she knew their contents by heart, could recite the promises they carried. Under other missives from friends and family was the envelope she was looking for.

Last week's unexpected note was from one of her former professors at the teachers' college. Irene had been pleased to receive it, then shocked once she'd read its contents.

An opening in the English department had been announced for next fall. One that Irene, according to her mentor, was very qualified for. It was only a junior instructor's position, but it would be a start.

The new faculty member would need to be settled in Cedar Falls by the end of July, at the latest. Was Irene interested? She'd excelled in her studies, and been well-respected by the professors and other students. It would be easy to put in a good word with the dean, and ...

Irene reread the letter, just as she had several times over the past few days. But slower, now; savoring every word of encouragement, every generous offer of assistance.

She wasn't going. Maybe Irene had known that, all along. Or maybe today, she'd turned a corner in her life.

She studied the cold fireplace as she turned the letter over in her hands. If she was the heroine of a melodramatic novel,

Irene would start a fire, rip the letter to shreds as tears streamed down her face, and toss the paper into the rising flames.

But she wasn't. And even though she wasn't going back to Cedar Falls, Irene decided she would keep this letter and treasure it always. It was a reminder of her potential. What she chose to do with that was up to her.

Maybe someday, it would be permissible for married women to teach school. Leo would support her, she was certain of that. And he was determined to start a seed-corn business on the side, as soon as they were settled. She could help with the books, create growth plans for the business. Maybe, just maybe, Irene could find fulfillment right here, at home.

Downstairs, someone was at the piano. The familiar notes of a holiday tune rose up the stairwell and crept under the closed door of Irene's room, and then she heard her neighbors lift their voices in joyful song.

Maybe she'd tell Leo about the letter; maybe she wouldn't. But after all these years of war and worry, Irene resolved to enjoy the here and now. She traded her skirt for a pair of comfortable trousers, and went to join the merrymaking in the parlor.

Tea Party
* 1956 *

Myrtle had the back yard to herself, thank goodness. Or at least, there were no other people lurking about.

A litter of young bunnies had appeared last week under the carriage house, and two of them were taking tentative turns around the garden on this refreshing April morning. A robin hopped about by the bird bath. The tulips in the carefully manicured beds along the back porch were awake, and showing off their shades of pink and yellow.

All this natural beauty, however, wasn't enough to calm Myrtle's nerves. She was in desperate need of a smoke.

She pulled a pack from the back pocket of her pedal pushers, glanced around her feet, and swore. Where was the old coffee can that she kept in the corner by the railing? Myrtle was careful to empty its ashes every few days, as she knew Edwin used it, too. Annie must have taken it out to the incinerator, and forgotten to bring it back.

Myrtle had to admit, Annie was a godsend. But sometimes, she couldn't believe she had hired help. She'd grown up in another of Eagle River's well-heeled families, but her mother had done nearly all the housework herself.

What else was there to do? Mother had always said. And now, as a young bride, Myrtle had to agree.

But Edwin's mother, Eleanor, had been horrified when

Myrtle refused to hire live-in maids.

When I took my place in that house, there were always at least three! You don't want to have your hair a fright and your nails chipped when Edwin gets home from the office.

While she didn't have a house full of staff, Myrtle had grudgingly submitted to one expectation put forth by this town's rather-thin upper crust. Last year, just months after her marriage, she'd joined the Eagle River Ladies' Aid Society. And this afternoon, promptly at two o'clock, Myrtle was hosting the club for the very first time.

Annie was usually gone by then, but Myrtle was paying her double her hourly rate today to hang around until five. Annie had been pleased, yet surprised, about the additional wages, as if she'd expected Myrtle to berate her into staying late without giving her a dime for her extra effort.

Well, Myrtle Bradford wasn't that sort of person.

"That sort of *lady*," she muttered as she lit her cigarette. She felt sorry for the tulips on the other side of the porch railing, really she did; but there was no time to track down the ash can. If she was careful, she wouldn't catch the flowers on fire. Coffee grounds were good for plants, right? Maybe a little ash in the soil wouldn't be so bad.

One puff, then another, and Myrtle felt so much better.

Smoking was rather crass, her mother always said. At least for women, and especially in public. It was different for the men, however ...

It's always different for them. Myrtle frowned as she inhaled again. *They get to go to the office, do interesting things. Come home to a spotless house.*

Myrtle wished she could go somewhere, and not just over to Peabody's lunch counter with some of the other young married girls. Or to the "book club" at the library, where few of the ladies bothered to read the monthly selections (*my headaches have been so terrible lately!*) much less have even one interesting thought to share.

She was going to drown in Eagle River someday, Myrtle decided as she leaned back against the porch railing. Not in the river itself (she wasn't *that* depressed) but in this town.

The one she'd come back to after four years of art school in Chicago. The one she'd promised Edwin, whom she'd known since she was twelve, was the only place she wanted to be. Here, with him and the brood of kids they would raise, living in his family's historic home on Oakland Avenue.

This massive house was a "wedding present" from the older generation of Bradfords, but Myrtle had always known it was more like a bribe. To make sure Edwin came home from his economic studies at the University of Minnesota; that he married the "right" sort of Eagle River girl (Myrtle was one of perhaps three that wasn't a shirttail cousin, her odds had been good); and that Edwin would take over his father's lucrative insurance business.

Myrtle's family was a shade less wealthy than the Bradfords. Her great-grandfather had started an ice-delivery business during the town's early days, and that had evolved into a successful trucking company as the decades rolled by.

While Edwin had his marching orders, Myrtle had been handed her own by her mother: Keep a spotless house; show up at every good-deed event in this community (there weren't many, it was too small); and join the aid society.

As a girl, Myrtle had never been quite sure what the club's members did, beyond gathering at each other's houses once a month to giggle, sip more sherry than tea, and gossip about everyone not in attendance.

Just one year ago, Myrtle had still been in Chicago, drinking espresso and more-potent libations with her art school friends while attending lectures and poetry slams. She'd graduated last May, as had Edwin. In mid-June, there'd been a lavish wedding here at the Lutheran Church and a reception at a dance hall in Swanton.

The newlyweds were sent off on a leisurely tour of

Europe, then came home in late July to find their belongings uncrated inside this massive house. His parents had moved into a "smaller" home down the street, but it was still a two-story house with enough bedrooms for several future grandchildren to spend the night.

Their mothers had even arranged the everyday furniture in the couple's new home, and had the workmen tuck everything else in some of the empty rooms. Other spaces had long ago been filled with relics from the Bradfords' deep roots in this town; Myrtle felt like she was living in a museum.

She and Edwin moved things around in the main areas to suit themselves, a small rebellion which had earned a few frowns from his mother but no outbursts of dismay.

"A lady never shows her true feelings," Myrtle reminded herself as she worked on her cigarette. "Never complain, never explain."

A moment later, she noticed movement beyond the far edge of the lawn. Mrs. Whitmore, who lived on the next street over, was hanging her washing on the line. The Whitmores weren't "old money" by Eagle River's slim standards, but Mr. Whitmore owned a car dealership on the south edge of town and Gracie was a member of the women's club.

Gracie's sharp gaze was trained on what was left of Myrtle's cigarette, and she flicked the damp towel in her hands with more aggression than was necessary.

Myrtle was certain her mother was about to get a near-breathless phone call, because such shocking news simply couldn't wait until that afternoon's meeting.

"Mrs. Bradford! Mrs. Bradford, come quick! Oh, I don't know what we're going to do!"

It still took Myrtle a moment, sometimes, to remember that Annie was talking to her. She'd asked Annie to call her by her first name, and Annie usually did. After all, Myrtle was only three years older than Annie. But in times of trial, Annie often forgot.

"Are you alright?" Myrtle called toward the open screen door as she rushed to crush her cigarette on the back sidewalk, then hurried into the kitchen. "Did you burn yourself?"

"Oh, I'm fine, ma'am. I mean, Myrtle." Annie's smile wavered. "But it's the napkins. We're seating sixteen today, but two of the beige ones are stained." Annie held up the offenders. "Something must have gone wrong after the New Year's dinner, even though I was sure I got all the spots out."

Annie gestured at the wooden case, which housed a smattering of other cloth napkins along with the beige set Myrtle and Edwin had received as a wedding gift. Myrtle would have loved to shock the society's ladies by handing out paper disposables, but expectations must be met. She considered the options, then had an idea.

"Let's use several colors! There are some light blue, and some sage green. We'll mix them with the beige, alternate them. They'll go perfectly with our spring theme."

Myrtle had shunned the idea of purchasing floral arrangements for this afternoon's event. The nearest flower shop was in Swanton, and this time of year they didn't have much more than carnations. Myrtle hated those; they reminded her of funerals. Instead, she'd clipped early blooming forsythia stalks from the garden for the receiving stand in the front hall, and styled vintage china bowls with shredded-paper "grass" and plastic eggs for the dining table.

"That will work!" Annie was clearly relieved. "But the other napkins haven't been used in a while, and there isn't time to wash them."

Myrtle held a few up for examination. "They're all clean. I'll just steam them with the iron."

That crisis had been averted, but the morning was ticking away. Along with finishing the food, they still needed to eat a quick lunch (Myrtle always joined Annie in the kitchen, who wants to eat alone?) and Myrtle needed to change her clothes.

"How are the cucumber sandwiches coming?" Myrtle knew they would be scrumptious, as Annie was very adept in the kitchen. Even so, she needed to distract her nervous helper from the near mishap of the cloth napkins.

"Those are done." Annie nodded proudly. "And on covered trays in the refrigerator. The scones are out of the oven, and the ambrosia salad won't take long."

Myrtle reached for the napkin case. "I'll arrange the table and get these freshened up. Maybe start frosting the petit fours? I'll help you when I'm done."

In the butler's pantry, she pulled the padded board down from the wall. While the iron heated, she went into the dining room.

The antique table had every leaf in it, and there was plenty of room for sixteen. Some of the club ladies had to rent tables when it was their turn to host, but the Bradfords' home came equipped with enough chairs, silver service, and matching china and glassware to entertain a crowd.

Myrtle's college years had been intended to be merely the equivalent of finishing school; instead, her classes had ignited an interest in interior design and decorating. She loved to draw and paint, and study home and garden magazines. Planning today's event, from the table theme to the menu, had been the highlight of her past few weeks.

But as she smoothed the ivory tablecloth and began to add the plates from the sideboard, Myrtle shook her head over the room's imposing damask wallpaper and the ornate curves of the chairs.

How she longed to transform this old house, bring it into the modern age!

Even if the front parlor's furnishings held fast to the past, the room would look so much better with its walls painted a soft peach. One day, she'd love to bring gallons of gleaming white paint home from the hardware store, and enlist Annie's help to erase the dark trim in some of the rooms.

But that wasn't going to happen. Myrtle knew the quarter-sawn oak casements and baseboards were worth far more than many of the vintage furnishings in this house, and that was saying something.

It was like this party, she decided as she added the cups and saucers, and made sure the forks and knives were even with the edge of the table. In Myrtle's life, and especially inside this house, tradition always seemed to have the upper hand.

Even so, she'd scored a few victories. In the back parlor, which was used as a casual living room, Myrtle had already booted the overstuffed pieces and added ones with clean lines. The formal rug there had been replaced by a casual jute one, and Eleanor hadn't commented on it … yet.

And last fall, Myrtle had ordered a pale-blue stove, decked out with chrome trim, when it became clear the old one was on its last legs.

It was the first major change she'd made to the house without consulting Eleanor. Edwin had only shrugged when Myrtle asked for his input, and said he wasn't going to wade into that fray.

Edwin was kind, and they'd known each other for so long; Myrtle knew she could have made a much-worse match. But sometimes, she wished her husband would show even a little interest in the parts of her life that happened when he wasn't around.

The doorbell chimed. "I'll get it!" Myrtle called toward the kitchen as she tossed her handful of teaspoons on the table.

The grandfather clock in the front hall said it was just after eleven. This guest had been expected, and he was right on time.

Myrtle felt the usual bubble of anticipation in her chest, but it was quickly deflated by its accompanying stab of guilt. Even so, her smile was wide as she opened the door.

"Mail for you, my lady." Brock Stevens presented her with

a stack of letters tucked inside a grocery circular. Their hands touched briefly, and Myrtle knew it wasn't an accident.

"Why thank you, sir. How kind of you."

Annie was still in the kitchen; Myrtle heard the clatter of trays and pans. She took a quick step forward, then shut the door behind her. They were alone, together, on the porch.

Brock wasn't from Eagle River, but he had family in the area. He'd finished his undergraduate studies at a private college two years ago, and had taken this job with the local post office to earn enough money for law school.

The Bradfords had long used the mailbox that was on a post along the front sidewalk, as the slot in the antique front door had been sealed decades ago. But Brock had brought Myrtle a package one day last fall, and they'd spent ten minutes visiting on the porch.

Now, as much as Myrtle hated to admit it, she looked forward to his arrival. Mondays, Wednesdays, and Thursdays; an occasional Tuesday or Friday. The doorbell never chimed if Brock happened to be working a Saturday, and that mail was always left in the box.

He was ruggedly handsome, with a strong build and sandy-brown hair. Myrtle could imagine him in a sharp suit, fighting for justice in a courtroom, as easily as he walked this section of Eagle River in his navy pants and tan button-down shirt.

She tried to discount the small pauses in their conversations, the invitation she often saw in Brock's blue eyes. All she had to do, Myrtle suspected, was say the right thing. Or rather, the wrong thing ... and everything would change.

But it wouldn't happen today. In just a few hours, the grand ladies of Eagle River would be appearing at this door. They would exclaim over the loveliness of Myrtle's home, then begin to repeat the bland niceties they recited to each other, month after month.

Brock and Myrtle had their own script, and she wasn't going to let this visit pass without enjoying it.

"You know," she teased him, "we do have a mailbox, there on the curb. You could always leave the mail in it. I thought to-the-door delivery was only for the old and decrepit. I have several years to go before I'm thirty."

Brock laughed, like always. "But that wouldn't be nearly as fun as getting to see you. How's the latest painting coming along?" Yesterday, they'd spent several minutes discussing modern art. "I can't wait for you to do something in the cubist style, and hang it in the parlor."

"I'm sticking with painting roses, for now," she admitted. "Perhaps a tulip or two, for contrast."

To Brock, she wasn't a daughter-in-law who needed to be brought to heel, a wife who waited in the day's margins for her husband to come home. Myrtle could count on Brock to not only show up, but to talk to her as an equal. Until he'd started doing just that, she hadn't realized how desperately she'd needed such a friend.

Besides, it was refreshing to see a new face in this town. Myrtle had lost touch with most of Eagle River's young people once she'd gone off to college. Of the classmates who'd been blessed with the same opportunities as Edwin and Myrtle, only a few had returned.

Myrtle glanced both ways up the street, and saw no one. Or at least, no one was out and about. But who might be peeking around their curtains, trying to see without being seen?

Edwin and Myrtle had given each other permission to see other people while they were separated during their college years. It had been Edwin's idea. They had their whole lives ahead of them, he'd said; and that way, they'd really be sure that each other, and the life waiting for them in Eagle River, was what they wanted.

Myrtle would always be glad she'd had a few other beaus

while she was away. Even so, she wondered why Edwin had suggested such a thing. And was he, even now, truly sure about the two of them? And, more importantly, was she?

"I should go," she told Brock with a resigned smile. "I'm hosting the ladies' club this afternoon."

"Yeah, I'd better move on." He laid a hand on Myrtle's bare forearm before turning away. "Have fun at your party."

"I'll see you tomorrow," she promised him. "I'll fill you in on who dropped her fork on the floor, and who scandalized the others by wearing her best winter hat to a spring tea."

With a laugh and a wave, Brock was gone. An acute loneliness settled over Myrtle as she watched him walk away. At the next house, and the next, Brock barely broke his stride long enough to drop his deliveries in the mailboxes.

Myrtle found Annie in the front hall, worriedly twisting a tea towel in her hands until it more closely resembled a rope. The historic home's front door had a tight seal, with only a small oval of glass near its top. Myrtle was fairly certain Annie hadn't overheard anything, much less saw anything.

Or was the blank expression on her face the one worn by servants when a situation required discretion?

"I pressed all the napkins, and the little cakes are frosted." Annie graciously omitted the fact Myrtle had plugged in the iron, then left it unattended. "What's next?"

Myrtle, in her own way, was wondering the same thing. For a very different reason.

"How about you start our lunch?" she suggested. "I'll finish the place settings, and we'll be just about ready."

✳ ✳ ✳

The spring air had turned humid; Myrtle just hoped her chignon would stay in place for two hours. Her girdle was cinched, and both crinolines were fluffed under her dotted-lawn dress. She looked like she'd stepped out of a fashion magazine, but Myrtle felt as one-dimensional as its pages.

"A society lady," she whispered as she turned in front of the full-length mirror, checked that her nylons' seams were straight. She certainly looked sophisticated, especially compared to her casual top and pedal pushers from that morning.

Myrtle wasn't sure how she felt about that. She was twenty-three; but the matron she saw in the mirror was at least a decade older.

She'd known most of the club's ladies, of all ages, most of her life. But something was different today. Myrtle wasn't just hosting the ladies' aid society for the first time; it was going to be the first of many. She could see herself five years from now, ten, even twenty; still in this house with Edwin; children arriving, growing up, moving out and possibly away.

And then she thought of Brock. Annie hadn't noticed anything, Myrtle was sure of it. Or, more like, the maid hadn't noticed anything other than the way Brock and Myrtle chatted on the porch, privately, several days a week.

Myrtle needed to be careful. Eagle River was a small town, with very few people in its top social tier. It wouldn't take much for someone to knock her off the pedestal she'd found herself on.

But it wasn't just this party, and Brock, that had her distracted. Over the past few months, as she'd studied her hometown through eyes that had seen more of the world, an idea had taken shape in Myrtle's mind.

Not everyone enjoyed the advantages she had always known. Too many, right here and elsewhere, were struggling. The Eagle River mill, which powered several industries along the river for nearly a century, had shut down two years ago. The brick factory provided more employment options for the region's laboring class, but it was rumored to close later this year.

The ladies' aid society prided itself on helping those who were less fortunate. But Myrtle saw an important, neglected need beyond its clothing drives, food donations, and other tokens of "assistance."

Education mattered in these modern times, and at a level that wasn't available in Eagle River. The high school didn't have a scholarship fund, and Myrtle wanted that to change. Today's meeting, here at her own home, was the perfect place to share her proposal.

As she hurried downstairs to help Annie with the last of the preparations, Myrtle reviewed her plan for this afternoon.

A handful of the older ladies, her mother and Eleanor included, tended to run these meetings the way they ran their own households: with a cool gaze and a rigid agenda. Myrtle hadn't requested time to speak, but she was determined to do so. At some point, when there was a lull in the conversation, she would propose her idea.

The food was now ready, the house was spotlessly clean. Myrtle and Annie took it all in for a moment, then gave themselves a brief round of applause.

"You've done an amazing job," Myrtle said as she removed the smock she'd tied over her party dress. "I couldn't have made this happen without your help."

"We're going to knock 'em dead, right?" Annie grinned as she put on a fresh, frilly apron. "Well, I mean, not until they've enjoyed their lunch. Because I can't wait to see the pleasant surprise on Mrs. Wheeler's face when she tries my ambrosia salad. I wish we'd been brave enough to make that quiche."

Myrtle laughed. "Maybe next time. There's only so much change these esteemed ladies can absorb in one afternoon."

The doorbell rang again; this time, Myrtle was intrigued. The club ladies, even the fashionably early ones, shouldn't arrive for at least twenty minutes.

But before she could reach the hall, Edwin's mother sailed through the front door.

"Where is your girl?" Eleanor whispered to Myrtle as she

adjusted her pillbox hat. "I waited and waited."

Members of the younger set were likely to remove their chapeaus in this unexpected heat, which was why Myrtle had decided to go without; but the old guard could be expected to keep theirs speared firmly in place.

"She's busy in the kitchen, Eleanor. Annie's worked especially hard for two days to help me get ready for the club."

"If you had more help, this wouldn't be a problem." Eleanor's gaze darted this way and that, as if checking everything was where it had been on her last visit.

"I want your opinion on the table decorations," Myrtle lied. "Let's go in through the front parlor."

She steered her mother-in-law in the opposite direction of the kitchen entrance at the end of the front hall. Annie was handling the pressure well, despite her angst over the napkins that morning. Myrtle was determined to keep the two of them apart as much as possible.

"Oh, my." Eleanor frowned slightly. "It's all rather ... colorful."

"Yes. It's for spring. I made sure to use the very-best china from the sideboard."

Eleanor leaned slightly toward the butler's pantry, another not-so-subtle attempt to ferret out exactly what Annie was up to in the kitchen. Eleanor wasn't early to be sociable, much less to help; she was here to evaluate and judge.

Myrtle couldn't take her out to the garden. There wasn't much to see, this early in the season, and the sun was hot. Besides, there was the little matter of the mashed cigarette butt still littering the back sidewalk.

And then, Myrtle had an idea. The club would consider her scholarship proposal today if she found a chance to mention it, but the ladies wouldn't vote on it until at least next month. In the coming weeks, Eleanor's opinion of the plan would be a significant factor in the older members' decisions.

"Let's sit for a moment." Myrtle pulled out two of the closest dining-table chairs. "I've had such a busy day; haven't you? And there's something I want to discuss before the meeting."

Myrtle walked through her proposal while Eleanor sat in silence. But the older woman frowned, albeit briefly, more than once.

"My dear, I don't know what to say," Eleanor finally said. "We already help ... those people. The club hosts several charity drives each year, as you know."

"But this is different!" Myrtle tried to keep the frustration out of her voice, but didn't quite succeed. "They need more than charity; they need a way to improve themselves, have more choices in their lives."

"You can't ask a leopard to change its spots," Eleanor said slowly, as if speaking to a child. "Their lives are all they know. What makes you think they want to change?"

"They have to change," Myrtle insisted. "We all do. The world is getting more complex. Technology is driving everything; it's not enough, anymore, to have a strong back and be willing to work hard. Education is the key."

"And what if they don't return?" Eleanor took another tactic. "Those people aren't of much help to this town if they move away. Myrtle, my dear, I don't know where you get these ideas of yours. College, I suppose."

Myrtle had expected this resistance. But she had one more card to play.

"You're only married into this esteemed family, just like me," Myrtle reminded her mother-in-law as Eleanor's eyebrows shot toward the ceiling.

"But we all know the story. How Clem Bradford, when he arrived in Eagle River, had limited prospects because he was unable to read or write. How Lena Baxter taught him his letters. How he saw all the opportunities here, and grabbed them with both hands."

Clem had invested in the land, made a fortune through buying and selling parcels while the town was young; then opened the region's first real estate office. His sons carried the business forward, and later expanded into the insurance market. Clem had designed this elegant home to be an enduring symbol of everything he'd accomplished.

"Eleanor, Clem Bradford started out in life as one of 'those people.' I think he'd be proud to have his name on a scholarship fund."

The women stared at each other for a moment across the corner of the dining table.

"Clem has been gone for over forty years, my dear," Eleanor finally said. "I met him once, briefly, as a young girl; you never did. I don't think either of us should be so bold as to speak on his behalf."

It was a firm "no," a response neatly tucked inside yet-another reminder of how young Myrtle was and how impulsive she could be.

Myrtle needed her mother-in-law's endorsement to get many of the club members on board, and Eleanor knew it. The power, as usual, rested in her lace-gloved hands.

And then, Myrtle realized, maybe it didn't.

Her father had given her a very generous sum when she'd married, and that money had remained in Myrtle's name only. Edwin had good-naturedly gone along with the idea, even though it was still unusual for a wife, or any woman for that matter, to have access to a bank account that wasn't managed by a male relative.

It was an advance on her inheritance, her father had told Myrtle, for her to use as she saw fit. "A little egg money for my girl," he'd said with a laugh, as if the grand windfall had been nothing more than a few bills and coins tucked away in a drawer.

Myrtle had also been given a chance to experience life far beyond Eagle River. Maybe she'd squandered her potential when she took the safe, easy route back to this town, but others were going to get their turn.

Forget the ladies' aid society; she'd talk to Edwin, instead. She wouldn't mention her misgivings about her life, even as she wondered if her husband had his own.

Edwin would surely see the value in starting a Bradford scholarship fund. But if he didn't, or he just didn't want to ruffle his mother's feathers, Myrtle would do it all by herself.

As she stared at her mother-in-law, Myrtle felt as if she was seeing Eleanor clearly for the first time.

The woman was so often cloaked in a resigned aura of suffering, as if her genteel life was almost too much to bear. And today, as the bright spring sunshine beamed in the dining room's windows, Myrtle noticed not only the still-delicate wrinkles on Eleanor's face, but the deep cracks appearing in her mother-in-law's armor.

No matter what happened in her life, Myrtle decided, she would never be like Eleanor. She would use her money to help others, and use her standing in this community to improve it and the lives of everyone around her.

The doorbell rang again. Neither of the ladies moved.

Then Eleanor sighed, and shifted as if to push back her chair. "Oh, that silly girl; I can't believe she didn't hear the bell. She's as useless as she can be."

The second Mrs. Bradford, the one now in charge of this house as well as her own life, was on her feet in a second.

"Don't get up." It was a command, not a request. "I'll answer the door. My guests are starting to arrive."

Seeds of Discontent
✳ 1982 ✳

The kitchen radio was still set to the station that broadcast the farm market reports. James must have had it on this morning, when he came in to get more coffee.

Lillian Duncan was about to turn the dial, but didn't. She needed to hear the latest updates, too; and better now than from James this evening. The sooner she learned what the futures markets were forecasting, the quicker she might formulate a plan to brace her family for what was coming.

"Forewarned is forearmed," she reminded herself as she took the pie dough out of the refrigerator. She'd already put away the rest of the chili from lunch, peeled the apples for the pies, and washed the dishes. It was better than letting them pile up; staying ahead was the smart thing to do.

Although these days, Lillian reflected as she scrubbed the counter and reached for the canister of flour, it was impossible to get ahead. They'd all tried that, the Duncans and their farming friends and neighbors, tried to expand as their industry continued to modernize. Did their best to meet the demand generated by all those agreements the United States had made with countries all over the world.

A global economy, they called it. Lillian knew it was important to change with the times; but what mattered most to her was what happened right here, in this farmhouse just a few miles west of Eagle River, and what happened to her neighbors, her community.

And this year's harvest, even though it wouldn't get rolling for a few weeks yet, was certain to be a bitter one.

As she dusted the counter with flour and reached for her mother's rolling pin, Lillian basked in the golden sunlight streaming through the kitchen windows. This old house had been here long before the Duncan family bought this land in 1928, but she loved its homey charm. James' parents, Edward and Doris, lived in the slightly newer home just up the road, and that was fine with Lillian. She'd grown up in a farmhouse just like this one, with small rooms and sloped upstairs ceilings, not ten miles from here.

This was home. And farming, as she and James reminded each other, especially when times were hard, was "all we'd ever wanted to do."

Fluffy, one of the barn cats, was strutting her way through a pile of early fallen leaves in the apple orchard just behind the house. It was a beautiful afternoon; but winter would be here all-too soon. How would they ever make it through?

Lillian tried to halt her circling thoughts by focusing on the first disc of pie dough. She noticed how quickly it warmed in her hands; felt how smooth its surface became as she rolled it thin, and then thinner; and admired the cobweb-like pattern of the flour as it was scattered on the dough. Her pies were legendary around Eagle River, thanks to her grandmother's crust recipe. The school's parent-teacher association was expecting two of them for tomorrow's bake sale, and Lillian wasn't about to shirk her duty.

As she rolled and rolled, she listened to the farm futures forecast. The announcer's chatty tone couldn't disguise the bad news he shared with his listeners. Corn: down; soybeans: down; hogs: up slightly, but forecast to drop again yet this week.

Out the other window, which focused on the gravel drive

that circled between the house and barn, she saw James, his brother, and his father roll the Duncans' best combine out of the machine shed and start to kick the tires.

Literally, at first. And then James went inside the shed, came out with two cans of machine oil, and handed one to Robert. Engines had to be calibrated, brakes had to be checked, and every other part evaluated so the machine was ready when the crops and the weather dictated it was time to harvest.

This newest combine was a deep green, and its finish sparkled in the early-autumn sun. How excited they'd all been when James brought it home from the dealership last year! One at a time, he'd taken Curtis and Elaine, and even Lillian, for a slow gravel cruise around the mile section.

The new combine was going to save time; and in the end, time was money. Even Edward, who remembered the Great Depression all-too well, had set aside his penny-pinching ways to marvel at how fast and efficient everything had become.

But lately, there'd been tension between father and son. Like most men, they didn't seem keen to talk about it; but Lillian knew this shiny machine and the hefty bank loan it had required was driving a wedge between James and his father.

The first pie crust was ready for the pan. As she draped it in and down, then trimmed the overhang and gathered the scraps for the next rolling, Lillian decided she couldn't listen to the farm station for one more minute.

She scrubbed her hands at the sink, turned the radio's dial until she found Loretta singing her latest "he done me wrong" country tune, and washed up again before turning back to her dough.

"How about a 'they've done us wrong' song?" Lillian muttered. "The government, the ag suppliers, the banks; every single one of them."

Foreign markets for American farm products were drying up faster than a corn field in a drought. The situation was complicated, and wouldn't settle itself overnight, but Lillian yearned for some sort of resolution. The prices farmers would get for these yields would be less than last year, and a fraction of what they'd been promised to be.

If they had to, the Duncans could sell that fancy combine. They wouldn't get what they paid for it, and that made Lillian smart with shame, but they could cobble together the cash to get the bank off their back.

The best thing they'd ever done was to refuse to buy that six hundred acres the Albertsons had for sale last year. An extra combine was one thing; a half-section of farmland, which required more seed, more taxes, more everything to make it pay, was a burden this family wouldn't have been able to overcome.

Some of their neighbors were far worse off, Lillian reminded herself as she reached for the crockery bowl filled with spice-dusted apple slices. Others hadn't just bought more machinery and land to meet an increased demand that was already ebbing away. They'd purchased more cows, more pigs. And for some, a new truck, a vacation to Florida. Even a new house. Those folks were the ones most likely to go under.

As always, Lillian hadn't exactly measured the ingredients for the pie crust. And she'd peeled and sliced all the apples from the basement bin that were just-right ripe today. There was enough of everything for a third pie, even if the top lattice would be a bit on the skimpy side. She pulled out another pie plate and went to work, because nothing at this farm ever went to waste.

Once all three pies were in the oven, Lillian reached for a cup of coffee and settled in at the table. The wonderful aroma of apples, cloves, and cinnamon soon filled the kitchen. She admired the dark wood cabinets, the red-checked valances over the windows, and checked the clock above the sink.

In twenty minutes or so, the school bus would roll down from the east and stop at the end of the Duncans' lane. The extra pie wouldn't be ready, of course, but there were oatmeal cookies in the jar if Curtis and Elaine wanted a snack before they started their chores. Supper would be leftover scalloped potatoes and ham, and a tossed-together salad, since the family would eat a bit early tonight. James was taking his turn on the Eagle River farmers' cooperative board, and their monthly meeting started at seven.

Those cookies were calling Lillian's name. While she enjoyed one and sipped her coffee, she flipped through the grocery ad that had come in yesterday's mail.

Feldman's Grocery had been on Eagle River's Main Street for several decades now. While it didn't have the wide selection of those fancy supermarkets in Swanton and Charles City, it carried most of what her family needed, along with offering a top-notch meat counter thanks to the family owned meat locker next door.

Thinking ahead to all the big meals she'd serve during harvest, Lillian was deep into her grocery list when she heard the squeaky springs of the enclosed back porch's door.

Seconds later, James staggered into the kitchen, his face pale.

"Oh no, what happened?" Lillian almost spilled coffee on the grocery circular as she bolted from her chair.

"It's my back. Again." James gritted his teeth as he unzipped his chore coat. When he grunted in pain, Lillian helped him free his arms. "Thanks, hon. Twisting around makes it worse."

"You really should go to the doctor, get it checked out. This is the second time in the last week."

"It's just a spasm." James went to the sink for a glass of water. But Lillian knew he was also trying to hide his pained expression from his wife for a few moments. "I was checking over the combine, and reached around too fast."

"Go lie down. I'll fetch the ice and the aspirin."

Lillian soon heard James moan as he lowered himself to the living-room floor. He insisted that laying flat-out on a hard surface was the quickest way to calm his back muscles, and Lillian went along with it. But the fact that her husband was trying to find ways to cope, rather than asking a doctor for help, was something they argued about.

James sighed with relief as Lillian slipped an ice pack into the just-right spot, then handed him the water and an aspirin. He tried to nod his thanks, but then winced. "I know what you're going to say. But I don't have time to go to the doctor."

"You don't have time for this, either." Lillian fetched a small pillow off the couch, but James shook his head.

"I just need a few minutes." James' voice was full of exhaustion as well as pain. It brought tears to Lillian's eyes. "I have to be in town before seven."

Elaine and Curtis soon arrived home from school. Curtis' concern for his father was matched by his excitement at this unexpected opportunity.

"Can I go out and help?" Their son loved nothing more than being outside with "the rest of the men," as he called them, even though he was fourteen. "I'll get my other chores done, too. I promise."

"You may." James issued his edict from the carpet. "But you need to do exactly what Grandpa and Uncle Robert tell you to do. And when you change out of your school clothes, be sure to put on your old overalls. Your mother does enough laundry, as it is."

Elaine brought her father an oatmeal cookie on a saucer. "Thanks, honey." James ruffled their daughter's dark-blonde curls. "I'll be ready for a snack soon."

It wasn't long before Elaine went out to feed the chickens, and Curtis was helping in the machine shed. Lillian checked on the pies, then went back into the living room. She lowered herself to the carpet, and stretched out next to James.

"Hey," he mumbled, "what are you up to?"

"Just wanting to spend a little 'quality time' with my husband. I'll take it when, and where, I can get it."

"You don't have to keep me company. I'll be alright."

"Eventually, sure. But for now, I'm going to stay right here with you."

Lillian stared at the ceiling plaster high over their heads. From this angle, she spotted a few cobwebs stretched across the tulip-shaped shades on the ceiling's fixture. "We have fifteen more minutes of peace, if we're lucky."

"Maybe twenty." Despite his pain, James chuckled softly. "Elaine loves those chickens, she's probably singing to them right now. And Curtis will 'help out' until Grandpa says it's time for supper."

"Can you imagine either of them being happy as a town kid?"

"Nope. And I would say the same about myself. And you."

"You know me well." Lillian turned just enough to smile at her husband, then rolled back.

James was right; there was something so supportive about lying on this farmhouse floor. She straightened her spine, and breathed deeply. "If you can't make it to the co-op meeting tonight, it'll be OK. I can call Fred, if you like."

Fred Bennet was the co-op's manager. While not a voting member of the twelve-man board, he was its secretary and the only staff person who attended their meetings.

"I suppose. Fred keeps the place spotless, as far as co-ops are concerned, but I can't imagine wanting to lie on that floor if my back starts to act up." James thought for a moment. "You know, maybe you won't have to call him. What if you go, instead?"

"Me?" Lillian raised her eyebrows toward the console television behind them. "You think I should go to the meeting?"

"You're good at those things," James reminded his wife.

"Why, you've run the women's circle at church, and the PTA fundraisers."

"Oh, I'm not afraid of speaking in public. I just don't see how it would matter, since I can't vote. They don't allow voting by proxy."

"I know, I know. But we have some important things to discuss after the meeting. Things that … aren't on the agenda. I have some notes written down; you could share my comments, at least."

James sighed. "It's bad around here, you know that. Everywhere else, too. And it's not going to get better. We need to be prepared."

Lillian felt the cold air from the cellar creeping through the worn floorboards and the thin padding on the back of the shag carpet.

"Tell me, James. Tell me what's going on."

So he did. More than once, he lowered his voice to a whisper even though they were still alone in the silent house, lying there on the floor. When he rambled to a stop, neither of them moved. They stayed right where they were, as the afternoon's sunbeams faded and shadows crept across the room.

"Oh, Lil," James finally said, the worry clear in his shaky voice. "What are we going to do?"

"I don't know." She turned his hand over in hers, touched the thick golden band on his ring finger. "I honestly don't know."

* * *

The co-op's parking lot was already packed by the time Lillian arrived. She was alone, but she'd brought reinforcements.

Two of the apple pies rested on a tray on the passenger-side floorboards, and a paper bag on the seat contained disposable plates and silverware. Fred might have napkins in the office, or she could snag paper towels from the restroom dispenser. She had no doubt there would be plenty of coffee.

James had felt well enough to join the rest of the family at the supper table, but promised Lillian he would rest most of the evening. Curtis would wash the dishes, and Elaine was already starting a pan of substitute brownies for the bake sale when Lillian left for the meeting.

It was an all-hands-on-deck night at the Duncan house, the sort of busy togetherness that Lillian would yearn for when both her children eventually left the nest.

But James had been right; tonight's co-op meeting was too important to miss. While she was still concerned about her husband's recovery, Lillian found herself eager to participate in tonight's discussion. After all, the trajectory set at this meeting would affect the farm wives around Eagle River, and their children, just as much as the men.

She'd accept a seat at this table, if only for one night. Perhaps she could do some good.

Tensions were sure to be high, compounded by the fact that the men were highly unlikely to show any vulnerable emotions while they debated the best way forward. Apple pie wouldn't fix the problem, but it might lower their boiling frustration to a simmer.

She was gauging the best way to get everything inside when Leo Shaw pulled in next to her truck.

"Why, Lillian!" Leo, who was in his mid-sixties, was the oldest current member of the board. He and Irene lived just a few miles from the Duncans. In such a rural area, this made them neighbors. "What are you doing here tonight? Where's James?"

Even in the dim parking lot, whose lights had just come on as the sun settled in the west, the confusion on Leo's face was easy to see.

He was a good man, kind, a World War II veteran admired by everyone he knew. Even so, the idea of a woman showing up at a co-op board meeting was just about more than Leo could comprehend.

"James is sick. Can you take this sack for me, please?" Lillian pushed it into Leo's arms without waiting for an answer. Given his state of shock, she wasn't about to let him carry the pie tray. "Thanks so much. Cut the first piece for yourself when we get inside."

In stark contrast to the vast lot and its rows of lofty grain towers, the co-op's office building was small and charming.

The red-brick structure had started out as an auto shop in the thirties. Beyond Fred's office, the front counter, and a few rows of merchandise, a door opened into two former garage bays.

On board nights, Fred shoved two long folding tables together in the first stall, and made it work. In the winter months, if the cold was especially intolerable, the men simply stood around the coffee pot in the shop's front corner.

Lillian could hear male voices and laughter before Leo opened the co-op's front door. They sounded suspiciously carefree; but Lillian suspected the chance to get away for an evening, especially this close to harvest, was a welcome opportunity for the guys.

All those conversations skidded to a halt when Lillian and her pies appeared.

"James' back is out," Leo reported before anyone could ask. "And Lillian brought us dessert."

That wasn't the half of it, but Lillian let it slide for now. "Where should I put these?" she asked Fred. "Are the tables set up in the back?"

He barely nodded, then followed her into the garage. "I don't know what to say, Lillian. The pies look wonderful, but this is a closed meeting. We don't ..."

She put down the tray. "I know, members only. And I know I can't vote by proxy for James." Lillian lowered her voice. "But that's not why I'm really here, Fred. I understand there are more important things to talk about tonight. James wanted to be sure his ideas were heard."

Fred stared at the garage floor. The men's voices and shuffling feet were getting closer to the other side of the door.

"I'm not leaving; the pies aren't a bribe so you'll let me stay," Lillian told Fred. "I only thought they might make things easier for all of you tonight."

"He told you … everything?"

"Yes. Now, where are the paper towels?"

To his credit, Leo cut many more slices after his own. He had the pie passed around by the time the coffee mugs were full. In Lillian's brief absence, someone had said something. She didn't know who, or what; but while the men still seemed guarded in her presence, they now understood why she was there.

Except for Oscar Tindall, who was known for his irascible attitude. The older man glared at Lillian from across the table; she stared right back.

"Women," Oscar muttered as Fred called the meeting to order. "They oughta be at home, washing the dishes."

Curtis hadn't balked when his mother had delegated that very chore to him tonight; Lillian was proud of that fact.

As Fred worked through the official agenda, Lillian studied the faces around this table. The board had a wide range of representatives these days, even if the ladies were still left out. Some of the men were like Leo, lifelong farmers nearly ready to retire. Others, like Tom Schupp, were just starting out. While most of them hadn't gone to college, Lillian knew Joe Koenig had an ag science degree under his belt.

Since she couldn't vote in James' place, Lillian stayed silent through the regular meeting. While the men groaned and shook their heads over the low prices the co-op would receive for this fall's crops, they accepted those proposals with rounds of dejected "ayes."

There was a brief debate over scaling back the number of part-timers the co-op had hired for the upcoming busy season. Donald Taylor reminded the rest of the board that those temporary employees, most of them high schoolers, took their pay home to their financially distressed families. Families who were members of this institution.

When Fred gaveled out the official meeting by slapping one palm on the table, the room fell into awkward silence. A few moments later, there was the screech of metal on concrete as Hiram Wheeler pushed back his folding chair.

"Well, I'll leave you boys to it." Hiram tipped the brim of his cap toward Lillian. "Ma'am."

The men's eyes followed Hiram to the office door, then made sure it had closed behind him.

"We'd better wait until you hear his truck start up," Joe warned the group. "I wouldn't be surprised if he's hanging around in there, trying to listen in."

"He'll stay out of it," Will Trowbridge predicted. "It's better for him if he's in the dark."

"He's a Wheeler." Joe stabbed his last bite of pie with his fork. "You can't trust any of them, not these days."

The Wheeler family ran the livestock auction barn in Eagle River, which also handled farm and estate sales. While Hiram farmed and wasn't directly involved in the business, his nephew, Marvin, was currently the company president. The Hartland County Sheriff had tapped Wheeler Auction Co. to run a sale two weeks from Saturday where the David Zimmerman family's entire farming operation would be up for grabs.

The Zimmermans had done too much, too quickly; and now, the banks were calling in their loans. Those acres had been in their family for four generations; but by the end of that afternoon, they'd be lucky to still own the house and the patch of yard that surrounded it.

Every cow and pig, every piece of machinery and every

vehicle they owned, was to be sold to the highest bidder.

"So, what's the plan?" Oscar asked Fred. "You want us to go around the table, see what we've got in mind? I'm happy to start."

Fred held up a hand. "You boys wanted to have this discussion, you do as you please." He glanced briefly at Lillian. "I'm trying to stay neutral here. Besides, it's better for everyone if we don't have any trouble."

"Trouble?" Leo leaned in. "Man, that's all we have. And it's only going to get worse." He looked around at his fellow farmers.

"The Zimmermans are just the first of us that are going to fail. You youngsters don't know what it was like in the thirties. I was just a teenager then, but let me tell you this: People took action. It was the only thing that worked."

"There's nothing wrong with arming yourself," Oscar told the group. "Me, I'm not showing up at that auction empty handed. If things go sideways, I'll be ready."

"I was talking about taking a stand," Leo clarified. "That's all. Violence isn't the answer."

"Sometimes it's the only way! I don't get it, Leo. You were in the war, you saw ..."

"I saw enough. Enough to last me a lifetime." The older man's hand trembled slightly as he lifted his coffee cup.

"We'll need to make our presence known," Will Trowbridge said, "push back against the sale. But it needs to stay peaceful." He leaned down the table toward Oscar. "What are you suggesting, anyway? You want a firefight? That'll backfire on us, on everyone. You want the National Guard called out, have them all up in our business?"

Oscar refused to soften his stance. "What are you so worried about, Will? Your family's in better shape than most. Leo, you're the same, thanks to that seed business you run on the side."

"A little pain might be needed to serve the greater good,"

Joe Koenig insisted. "The politicians, the bankers ... they don't give a damn about us little guys. We need to get their attention! This isn't about David Zimmerman, it's about all of us. He'll get over it, whatever happens."

Donald stood up, his pie unfinished, and started for the door. "I'm done. No more of this. I can't ... I don't want anything to do with it."

After Donald left, the men stared into their coffee cups, at the crumbs on their paper plates, at their hands. Anywhere but at each other.

"What?" Joe finally asked. "What did I say?"

Lillian thought she knew. The Wisconsin farm of one of Donald's cousins had fallen into foreclosure. The day before the auction, his cousin hadn't come in for breakfast after morning chores. His wife and children, who were gathered around the table, heard the shotgun blast. She'd found her lifeless husband in the hayloft.

Lillian looked around her, at so many men she'd known for most of her life, and wondered how her community could find a way through this crisis.

"What I think we need to do," Lillian said slowly, "is to show strength in numbers while not causing anyone, including all of us, more harm."

Pete Langstrom, one of James' closest friends, gave her an approving nod from across the table. James had promised Lillian that he and Pete were on the same page.

"I'm sure some of you've heard about the penny auctions during the Great Depression," Pete told the group. "The crowd, or the majority of it at least, was in agreement to keep the bids low, ridiculously low. Farmers were assigned items to bid on, so there wouldn't be any competition. And they only spoke up once the suggested price had dropped way down from a lack of takers."

Lillian had James' notes in her hands, but she didn't need them. "Some of the items would go as no-sales," she explained. "The ones that managed to get a bid would be handed back to their owners."

She looked at several of the men in turn, then focused her gaze on Oscar Tindall. "But it only works," she said, "if everyone agrees to participate. If everyone is on the same page."

"I've been thinking the same," Ryan Hinton said. He was one of the younger men on the board. "The bank has to take what they can get, and no more. We can put those loan sharks in their place, screw them over without letting the situation deteriorate into violence."

Will nodded in agreement. "It's going to take some serious planning. Who bids on what, at what price; how the items are transferred back to the Zimmermans."

"Are they going to pay us back?" Joe was skeptical. "I mean, they're broke; that's the problem."

"Maybe," Leo said. "Maybe not. Maybe you just take it on the chin, give someone else a little grace. Because let's face it: The Zimmermans aren't the only ones who are going to go through this. You never know when it's going to be your turn."

Oscar was about to say something; by the smirk on his face, Lillian knew it wasn't going to be productive.

"We can't solve this tonight," she said quickly. "Go home, talk to your wives. Think about what you are willing, and not willing, to do."

"You have my number," Pete told the rest of the board. "Let me know what you decide. If you don't feel comfortable participating, that's fine. And if you know someone who would want in on this, and they can be trusted to stay quiet about it, have them call me."

* * *

When the meeting broke up, the men were as silent as they'd been sociable before it started. Fred waved away

Lillian's offer to help clean up, and she was soon back in the truck with just two slices of apple pie left.

Once she left Eagle River, the darkness pressed in around her. Her truck was alone on the highway west of town, and it was the same once she turned off on the gravel.

Driving solo, whether she was piloting a combine through the fields or heading into town to run errands, had always helped Lillian work through any problem at hand.

It gave her mind the quiet space it needed to focus her thoughts, and sift through them to consider what she could, or should, do.

She couldn't begin to solve this crisis; it stretched from one end of the country to the other. But here, in Eagle River, could she find a way to make a difference?

Organized resistance at the farm auctions was a good idea, if it was done right; but it wasn't going to be enough. This wasn't just about not having enough money, or too much debt, or staggeringly high interest rates. For these farmers, including her own family, the loss of their land would be a heartbreak that would never really heal.

But too many people, especially the men, couldn't put their feelings into words. They wouldn't ask for help; they would try, and fail, to carry their burdens alone.

Lillian thought of Donald Taylor's cousin, his wife, and their children; and then, she recalled the look on Donald's face when he'd bolted from the meeting. There had been no tears, no sadness. His expression had been the opposite: empty of any emotion at all. Numb, cold.

And then there was Oscar Tindall, always so cantankerous and rude. Lillian occasionally ran into his wife at the grocery store or the pharmacy, and hadn't been able to overlook how the poor woman tried to hide the bruises on her face and arms.

"When the shock wears off, the anger will set in." Lillian slowed for a rural crossroads, then rolled through it. "That anger needs to be let out, in a safe way; and the grief has to be shared, somehow."

There needed to be a clinic, Lillian decided as she turned up her farm lane. Somewhere people could go, have someone to talk to. She didn't know where to start, or how. But her sister was a nurse; maybe Joanne would have some ideas. The counseling had to be affordable, yet not necessarily free. Most people around here were too proud to accept anything that hinted at charity.

James was haunting the kitchen, waiting for her return. His back was feeling better, he said; he'd be back at it in the morning. Lillian was too preoccupied, and too tired, to have that debate tonight.

"How did it go?" he asked anxiously. "Did the guys come to a consensus on anything?"

Elaine, who was watching television in the next room, could hear every word of this conversation.

"Not yet," Lillian told her husband, then cut her eyes toward the living room. James understood; they would talk later. "But there was some productive discussion, at least. And there's pie left," she added brightly. "Two pieces."

"Curtis is upstairs, doing homework," James told his wife as he dished up a slice of apple pie. He paused long enough to give her a quick kiss. "Thank you," he whispered.

"Glad I could help," she whispered back.

Part of Lillian wanted to tell James about her idea, along with what happened at the meeting; part of her had to acknowledge it was too new, and too big, to put into words just now. She would talk to Joanne tomorrow, and go from there.

The door to Curtis' room was cracked open, lamp light spilling out into the hallway.

"Hey," Lillian said to her teenage son. Then she chuckled. "Dad says homework is being completed up here. I'm not sure that counts."

Curtis lowered his magazine, which was James' latest issue of a popular agriculture periodical. "It's all done. I've moved on to something more interesting. You know I'm going to be a farmer, just like Dad, and Grandpa and Uncle Robert. After college, of course."

"Yes, after college." It was a conversation they'd had many times before.

Lillian gave her son a smile she didn't feel. He was so determined, so sure of his future. She hoped his dream could still come true when all this was over.

"Well, then." Lillian patted the open door's frame, as her son had insisted several months ago that he was too old for goodnight hugs and kisses. "Be sure to turn out your light when you turn in."

Night Watch

* 2009 *

Raindrops splattered the cruiser's windshield as Police Chief Wade Friese waited at Eagle River's lone stoplight. It was a Saturday night in March, a time of year when it was a toss-up whether it was winter or spring.

A battered maroon pickup rolled up on Wade's right. He knew who was inside before he even checked the license plate.

"Rob must be taking it easy tonight," he muttered as Rob Wellman's truck started over the bridge. It moved on at 24 miles an hour, according to the cruiser's radar, in a nearly perfect straight line. "Maybe that drinking and driving course sobered him up for good."

Even as he uttered it, Wade knew that wasn't likely. Sometimes, people were able to turn a bad situation around, at least for a while; especially if they had something, or someone, motivating them to do so. But unfortunately, that often didn't last.

Wade was glad Rob was behaving himself tonight, at least. Sure, the police chief did the right thing when it was required; but he'd rather help some elderly woman carry her packages, or chat with the teens in the school parking lot before class, than slap the cuffs on a fellow resident and corral them in the back of his squad car.

He turned south on Main Street, and a rumble of thunder soon made him punch the "call" button on his radio. "Jeanie, what's the latest forecast? Are we getting heavy rain overnight?"

"Looks like a band moving in over you in the next ten minutes or so," the dispatcher reported. "It's passed through here, already. You're alone for at least a few more days, right?"

"I sure am. Tom's out of town until Monday."

"Jeff Preston's one of the deputies on duty tonight. He's in your neck of the woods if you need a hand."

That made Wade grin. He didn't expect trouble, but you never knew what might happen. Jeff was a seasoned Hartland County deputy, and had an excellent track record along with being one of the local boys. "Thanks, Jeanie. I'm glad to hear that."

Main Street was quiet, which was typical for Eagle River when the midnight hour rolled in. Only the Eagle's Nest, that new sports bar, was packed with people. Wade was pleased to see the place so busy. He'd been chief here eight years, but could count on one hand the number of new businesses in that time. And it only took two fingers to acknowledge which ones were still open.

There were so many dark storefronts, beyond a few security lights here and there. So many blank windows. The 1980s farm crisis hit this little town hard, like it had so many. Eagle River had lost its grocery store, even though the meat locker managed to stay in business. There was just one gas station now, which was part of a chain, rather than two local options. People were driving farther to find work, and they often shopped where they were employed. And then, of course, there was the internet.

And with a recession now bearing down on this country, the somewhat better times of the past twenty years looked like they were on their way out.

"It's a good thing they started that community counseling clinic in the eighties," Wade mused as he rolled into the next block. The center was housed in an old storefront, and staffed three days a week with a rotation of psychologists from around the region. They donated their time to connect people with the resources they needed.

The program, which was started by a handful of farm wives and members of the medical community, had been far ahead of its time.

Especially in a remote area with fewer resources, where emotions were more likely to be smothered than shared. Too often, as all law-enforcement officers knew, the anger and pain came out through someone's fist, was poured into a bottle, or pushed down with a pill.

The police chief drove around to the back alley, and parked behind the medical office that was next door to the counseling center. Doctor Murray was vigilant about keeping his small practice locked and the alarms set when it was closed, but Wade and Tom always checked that everything was as it should be.

Three weeks ago, the doctor's office had been burglarized. Murray had been forced to order a custom-sized window to replace the broken one, due to this old building's unique design, and a piece of plywood still covered the hole.

The would-be thief had been too high to easily find his way around the clinic in the dark, and was still trying to pry open the locked storage room with a crowbar when Officer Tom Peterson arrived. While the burglar (and his lawyer) continued to deny it, Wade was sure the young man had been after the prescription painkillers Murray had in his clinic.

Eagle River's pharmacy was where the lion's share of the legal drugs were kept in this town, and everyone knew it.

But the addicts also knew that Chris Everton, who'd taken over the business just last year from his longtime mentor, had his Main Street building locked down like Fort Knox. Chris had even installed one of those fingerprint-scan systems on the pharmacy's storage room door, ensuring that only himself and the assistant pharmacist had access to what was inside.

The rain was coming down heavily now, just as Jeanie said it would; but Wade reached for his flashlight and got out to check that the medical clinic's back entrance was secure. He spent a few more minutes shining the beam up and down the alley, which had no lights of its own.

Soaking wet but satisfied that nothing was amiss, Wade returned to his cruiser. It was only then that he realized he should've let Jeanie know he was getting out of the car. The alley was pitch dark; someone could have been hiding in the shadows.

Back in the day, especially in a town this small, officers would have thought nothing of what Wade had just done. But now, police departments of every size were reporting more instances of disrespect and outright hostility from the public. Sadly, too many of those folks were high on one thing or another.

And that was the reason Chief Friese had checked the alley so carefully. Someone loitering there could have posed a threat, but they may also have needed assistance. Drugs had always been around, in Eagle River and everywhere else, but they were gaining a bigger foothold in the small towns these days. One that Wade suspected would only grow as the economy faltered.

Opioid abuse was the latest layer to the problem. "But the weed never went away," Wade reminded himself, quoting one of his academy buddies, "and the meth is here to stay."

Wade turned back out onto Main Street, and headed north over the main bridge. Peabody's Restaurant was dark, but secure; it was the same for the auction barn across the street.

The convenience store closed at midnight, and the Eagle's Nest and Paul's Place at two. If it was still quiet around one, he'd head home to Colleen and the boys, knowing that Jeanie would radio him if anything came up. In the meantime, he'd check the young people's usual gathering spots.

There wasn't much to do in Eagle River, especially this late. Field parties were common but always outside the city limits, so those were monitored by the sheriff's department.

A few older teens were cruising Main Street, but it wasn't much fun when it was raining, and chilly, and you didn't have much company. Wade interrupted two young lovers in a car in the library's parking lot, then found his way to a loosely organized party on the front porch of one of the rentals just west of the business district.

A row of these once-grand houses had been chopped into apartments a few decades ago. It was a shame, in a way; but they offered reasonable rent for working-class folks who were barely hanging on. The housing market bubble had burst last year, and Wade worried more of the town's larger homes might eventually succumb to the same fate.

A few kids at this porch party were too dumb, or too drunk, to ditch their cans before Wade caught them with beer in their hands. Citations were issued, parents were called, and Wade gave a lecture to the weary-eyed mom upstairs whose son had organized tonight's social event.

A second gathering, just down the street, was more subdued. Wade didn't find any alcohol, and the ones smoking cigarettes were old enough to do so. But the teens' bored stares, the slump of their still-young shoulders, caught the police chief's attention. In a few years, some of them would flee this town. Some who stayed would build solid, productive lives; but others were certain to struggle.

Wade took the time to chat with these kids about school and sports and whatever else reminded them that he, Police Chief Friese, was their neighbor and friend. Even so, Wade wondered which of them his department would eventually charge with drug possession.

There was one more hangout that Wade wanted to check, even though it was an inhospitable spot on a cold, damp night like this one. He pointed his cruiser east, and headed for the train trestle over the river.

The railroad's arrival had made this town thrive, long ago. But as the world changed, passenger cars eventually stopped coming through Eagle River. Even the local co-op moved its products by truck these days.

This rail line had changed hands many times over the decades, and the last owners decided about five years ago to abandon this stretch of track.

The Eagle River Historical Society hoped to turn the long-shuttered depot into a museum, or at least get it placed on the National Historic Register, but Wade couldn't imagine where they'd find the money. There'd been talk about the county taking over the abandoned railroad bed, turning it into a bike and nature trail. While that seemed more likely, those improvements might be a long time coming.

So for now, the section of exposed riverbank under and around the trestle was mostly populated by partiers at night, and occasionally fishermen by day.

Those casting lines were sometimes joined by nature enthusiasts, as Eagle River's majestic namesake birds had returned a few years ago after a several decades' absence. The two nests on the far side of the river were now guarded by eagle parents watching over their eggs.

Second Street's pavement turned to gravel past the last house and final streetlight. The cruiser's headlights soon swept over the brambles and trees that separated the narrow road from the mighty river.

At the bottom of the slope, Wade reached for his radio. This was one place he never forgot to share his whereabouts with dispatch when he got out of the car. He cinched his parka hood, checked his walkie-talkie and sidearm, and picked up his largest flashlight.

The rain had slowed to a steady drizzle, but the cold wind was relentless when he left the shelter of the woods. The trampled footpath that led to the river's edge was slick and fringed with ice, and he carefully picked his way toward the roar of the rushing water.

In the dark, Wade felt, rather than saw, the trestle looming overhead. Its massive timbers' wide shadows had created a dirt beach where even tenacious grasses and trees refused to grow. The clearing was muddy tonight, and Wade wasn't surprised as his light swept the underbelly of the trestle and confirmed he was alone.

The river was high and wild, full of snowmelt as well as rain. Most of it ran free, but there were still jagged chunks of ice trapped in pockets along the water's edge and jammed against the trestle's legs. The ice rocks shifted and cracked under the pressure of the current, and their creaks and groans echoed through the river bottoms.

As he turned away from the water and back toward the comfort of his cruiser, Wade's flashlight picked up on something in the mud.

It was a syringe, dirty and used, with a spot of dried blood still clinging to the tip of its needle.

Wade had been prepared to find something like this. With a sigh that was instantly carried away by the relentless wind, he yanked on a set of disposable gloves and pulled a small trash bag from his coat pocket.

✳ ✳ ✳

She might as well get out of bed, Colleen decided. She'd been tossing and turning for an hour, already; it was a poor way to start her stretch of time off from the hospital in Swanton. Colleen wasn't back in the nurses' rotation until seven Tuesday morning and, if Eagle River stayed quiet, she and Wade might be able to relax this weekend.

Spring break was only a week away; that didn't seem

possible with clumps of dirty snow still lining the streets and a cold rain drumming against the windows. Theresa, who was away at college in Iowa City, was coming home for a few days. Kevin, their youngest, would start little league practice soon after. And Eugene, their oldest son, would graduate from high school in May.

Colleen should be excited about what the coming weeks would bring. But tonight, all those future milestones had been pushed to the back of her restless mind.

She checked the clock as she entered the silent kitchen, which was lit by only the light over the sink, and looked at her cell phone one more time.

No texts, no calls. Eugene had blown off his curfew again. This was the fifth time since the holidays, and the second weekend in a row. It was now after one in the morning, and her oldest son still wasn't home.

Colleen didn't want to turn on the overhead light. She didn't want to distract Kevin if he got up to use the bathroom. And there was comfort to be found in the cozy kitchen's shadows.

She almost reached for three mugs, then decided on two. Next came the bread, and peanut butter and jelly. Wade was likely to be hungry when he got home, and a warm, toasted sandwich would hit the spot. It was too late for coffee, at least for her husband; Wade would probably decide on tea before he took a shower and went to bed.

But Colleen pulled out the instant coffee as she waited for the microwave to heat her mug. Her night watch was just getting started. She'd stay up until Eugene came home.

Their ranch on the south side of town wasn't fancy. It had been rather cramped, to tell the truth, when five of them had been packed inside its walls.

Theresa's bedroom was vacant now, but she came home often enough that her parents hadn't wanted to reclaim that room quite yet. The boys had shared a bedroom until Eugene turned thirteen, and then he and Wade had made over a basement storage room into a cool teen cave. Colleen had tried not to roll her eyes about the glow-in-the-dark paint her oldest son had wanted on one wall.

"We'll redo this after he moves out," Wade had told his wife with a grin. "Maybe turn it into a sewing room for you."

Toenails echoed off the dining room's hardwood floors as Goldie left her dog bed and aimed for the living room and the front door. Their Lab mix wasn't as steady on her feet as she used to be, but her hearing seemed as good as ever.

"Who's here?" Colleen called softly to the dog, whose nose was now pushed between the picture window's closed curtains. "It's Dad, I bet."

Colleen always breathed a sigh of relief when Wade returned from yet another shift in good shape. Even better, tonight's timing might offer a lesson to Eugene. If his father, the town's police chief, made it home before he did on a Saturday night, might that tell the teen something important?

Wade soon came in, tired and cold. He nodded to his wife, and gave Goldie some loving attention before he started to remove his soggy outer layers.

"How was tonight?" Colleen asked from behind the rim of her steaming mug. The caffeine was already hitting her system, she could feel it working. Good; she was going to need it.

"Pretty quiet. Some business checks, a few underage drinkers." Wade set his work stuff on the far end of the kitchen counter, rather than one of the kitchen table chairs. Because even in her old age, Goldie was a curious dog.

"Peanut butter and jelly!" He grinned at his wife. "You know what I like."

"There's fried chicken in the fridge, too," Colleen said. She paused, almost afraid to ask the question that loomed large in her mind. Waited to see if her husband would offer the information she yearned to know.

"I didn't see him," Wade finally said as his toast popped up. "I kept an eye out as I made the usual rounds. Even went down to the trestle, though it's a terrible night for a party down there."

He took his usual chair at the table. "I'm guessing you haven't heard from him since I texted you last?"

Colleen could only shake her head.

"What are we going to do?" Wade wondered around a mouthful of his sandwich. "There are only so many punishments we can hand out that'll matter. He sneaks out even when he's grounded."

"We can't fully take away the car. He's Kevin's wheels to get to practice, sometimes; that's not feasible even if we made them both walk to school for the rest of the year."

Wade closed his eyes for a moment, ran the numbers. "Twelve weeks is all that's left. But then, there's summer, too. Come late August, Eugene will up in Decorah, at college."

Colleen hated the thought of another child leaving the nest, but she was especially worried that Eugene wasn't mature enough to handle all the freedom college would bring. Even so, he was near the top of his senior class, a shoo-in for one of those Bradford scholarships.

The awards wouldn't be announced until Senior Night in late April, but Wade and Colleen were counting on that money to make their own stretch a little further.

Eugene had been interested in engineering since he was a young boy; the program at this private college was outstanding.

It would be a bit more expensive than a public university, even with an aid package, but Wade and Colleen had agreed a smaller school might be a better match for Eugene. Perhaps he'd settle down there, focus on his studies.

Their son's other love had always been automobiles. He and Wade had purchased Eugene's sedan together; then fixed it up, side by side, in the garage.

"I'm starting to wonder about this fall," Colleen said to her husband. "I know Eugene loves engineering, but it's a competitive program. What if he's taking on too much?"

"I've been thinking the same," Wade admitted. "He's a genius with cars; there's no shame in working with your hands."

Colleen was glad they were on the same page. "We have a few more weeks before a final decision must be made. And there are several excellent tech schools to consider."

"That Bradford scholarship isn't just for four-year colleges, right?" Wade asked before taking another sip of his tea.

Colleen nodded. "Myrtle and Edwin were clear about that when they started the endowment fund, all those years ago, and the governing board has stayed true to their wishes."

"Let's talk to him about that when we settle on the punishment for tonight's infraction. His future is out there, somewhere. Maybe if we tie the two together, it'll help him see the big picture."

"He could start with general courses, wherever he goes," Colleen suggested. She already felt better about the situation. "Take things one step at a time."

"That's always the best way, in my opinion." Wade drained his mug, then looked across the table at his wife. "I can stay up and wait for him."

"No, no." She waved Wade off. "You've had a long night, even if it was quiet. I was sound asleep until a few minutes ago," she lied. "I want to be the one to 'welcome' him home."

Her sarcastic tone brought a chuckle from Wade. "I'll leave you to it, then. We'll regroup as a family tomorrow."

"What's the saying? 'Hell hath no fury like a mother who has to wait up for her son?' I'll promise to keep it quiet, though, so we don't wake Kevin."

Wade gave her a kiss, then headed for the bathroom. Goldie followed, and Colleen heard her settle on the floor outside the closed door as the shower came on. Fifteen minutes later, Wade was in bed and, Colleen hoped, would soon be fast asleep.

Goldie padded back out into the kitchen. "It's just us girls now, huh?" Colleen rubbed the dog's back. "It'll be two o'clock before we know it. If you get tired, go lie down. I can handle this shift on my own."

She had to. In truth, she wanted to.

Colleen had been nothing short of relieved when Wade had decided to call it a night. That he had bowed out until morning, when everyone would be rested and could see things more clearly.

What Wade didn't know, what Colleen had yet to tell him, was that she already saw everything as clear as day.

And it was far worse than they'd suspected.

She'd known it since this afternoon, when she'd come home from the hospital and the boys were still at school. She needed to start some laundry, and had gone into her oldest son's room. When she'd pulled the sheets off Eugene's bed, Colleen found a baggie of pills stuffed between the mattress and box spring.

Such a common spot to hide them, she'd thought as she held the bag up to the dim sunlight streaming in the egress window. *It's almost as if he wanted me to find these.*

And then, another thought hit her with so much force that she'd had to sit down to catch her breath: *My son is an addict.*

There was no note taped to the bag, nothing that gave anything away. But Colleen, who'd been a nurse for more than twenty years, knew exactly what was in those pills.

They were the ones everyone wanted these days, out on the street. The ones that were still being handed out by well-meaning doctors worried about their patients' comfort, and by shady pharmacists who didn't give a damn about anything but making some fast money under the counter.

Where did he get them? Who gave them to her son?

But, most importantly: What was she going to do about this?

For a few minutes, Colleen had assumed she'd tell Wade first. They were a team, they faced every crisis together.

And then, she hadn't been so sure.

It wasn't just that her husband was the police chief in their small town. That it'd be the talk of Eagle River if Wade had to arrest his own son for illegal possession of opioids. (Could Wade even do that, as Eugene's father? Would Tom have to do it?)

It was that her son, despite keeping late hours and having to shave every day, was still a boy. Eugene was seventeen, and would be for almost four more weeks. Getting caught now would be a problem, but his record would be expunged when he became an adult. If he didn't stop, if he was arrested even one month from now, it would haunt him the rest of his life.

Colleen wasn't angry with her son; she was furious. She would not let this stand, would not let Eugene throw his future away for a high.

There would be consequences. Tonight.

Even now, she wasn't sure exactly what those would be. But her message to Eugene would be clear: *You and I clean this up together, right now, and your father won't have to get involved.*

Would that threat work? Colleen didn't know. And if Eugene started yelling, if she started yelling back, the whole house would be wide awake and the pills would be out of the bag, so to speak.

She'd start out slow, careful, calm. *Let's sit at the table for a moment,* she'd tell her son as she studied his eyes, his gestures, and tried to figure out if he was high. *Have some coffee with me. We need to talk.*

Even if Eugene agreed to stop, even if he told her how he got the drugs (should she even bother with that tonight?) how would she ever know if her son was telling the truth? How could she police him, every hour of the day and night? She couldn't.

She'd first put the pills in the pocket of her jeans, then transferred them to her robe at bedtime. As she sipped her coffee, her other hand checked her left pocket for reassurance the baggie was still there. Colleen loathed having the pills in her possession, having these evil things in her house; but she clung to the false hope that if she kept them close, she could stop the damage they'd already inflicted.

Colleen knew she was betraying Wade's trust in her by doing this alone. He'd say it would make things worse for him professionally if this ever got out, that this had happened in his own home and he hadn't done the right thing by the law.

But if she kept it from him, and he didn't even know about it, who could say he'd been in the wrong? All the blame would fall on her.

That was another worry, one that weighed on Colleen as she nibbled a piece of peanut-butter toast and watched the clock.

What she was about to do, especially if she let it go on for too long, had to be some sort of crime. Having knowledge of a criminal situation, and not reporting it. Was it aiding and abetting? Obstruction of justice? Colleen wasn't sure, and wasn't about to turn on the computer to look it up.

Eugene was what mattered, more than anything. Her son was her only concern, at least for the next four or five hours, until a new day arrived and Colleen had to face what she'd done, or not done.

Colleen was tired. She was beyond tired, truth be told; she was out on some sort of emotional ledge, an uncharted place where fear, anger, and frustration surged through her body along with the caffeine.

But then, wasn't this what every mother faced, at some point in her life? And more than once?

A nearly impossible decision had to be made; one with several options, but each as complicated as the last. No one there to tell you what was right; or even if there was a way out, some sort of peace on the other side of this moment.

Life was hard; it had always been this way.

Especially for us women, Colleen thought as she sat there in the half-dark of her own kitchen, the rain still running down the windows and a cold wind whistling in the chimney. While she stared at the wall and waited for her son to come home, Colleen's mind wandered to other hard times she'd known, and how she'd managed to get through them.

And she was far from the first person called to meet life's challenges head on. The women in her family had always been the keepers of the secrets. The ones to take action; whether on their own, with each other, or with their husbands.

And then, from seemingly out of nowhere, Colleen remembered an old, passed-down story she'd heard about one of her great-great-great grandmothers.

Violet Hendricksen had come to Eagle River as a young bride. Her first baby, a daughter, died only minutes after being born. Haunted by her baby's death and terrified of the wolves that roamed in and around the village, Violet had passed many nights on the hillside where her daughter was buried, a hunting rifle in her lap.

Violet demanded the town's leaders build a fence around little Amelia's grave. An impressive amount of money was raised; several sections of iron fence, far beyond what was needed to protect Amelia's resting place, arrived by train.

A handful of the women, with Violet among them, soon formed the Eagle River Cemetery board. They made sure the plot was neatly mowed, its fence maintained, and the personal details of those buried there recorded for posterity.

Violet and Joseph raised seven other children to adulthood, but she still found time to give back to her community. She was a longtime member of the ladies' aid society, and volunteered with several other organizations that helped those in need.

As she pondered Violet's determination, Colleen hoped she'd inherited even a little of that woman's iron will. She soon realized, however, there was one very important difference between herself and her ancestor.

Violet hadn't been able to save little Amelia, but Colleen could still save Eugene. It wasn't too late.

Her second cup of coffee was nearly gone by the time headlights once again glowed through the picture window's curtains. Colleen's fear, and most of her anger, had drained away.

Maybe it was just all the caffeine, or maybe it was more. But her mind was focused, prepared. Ready to take on whatever happened in the next few minutes.

Goldie raised her head and thumped her tail. Under the pitter-patter of the rain, Colleen heard her son's car power down in the driveway. She pushed back her chair, adjusted the belt of her robe, and squared her shoulders.

"He's home," she told Goldie. "Let's meet him at the door."

Connections

There are plenty of twists and turns in these tales, and countless threads that tie these people and places to the "Mailbox Mysteries" series. Some might be obvious to an eagle-eyed reader, while others are so slight as to be nearly invisible. How many of these did you find?

(Non)spoiler alert: Don't worry, none of these tidbits are clues to the mysteries Kate Duncan and her friends unravel within the book series.

We Will Cross Here: 1858

The Baxter family, which eventually started the bank in Eagle River, plays a prominent role in many of the novels. It seemed fitting to start with their arrival.

We're repeatedly told in the books that Roberta Schupp, the town's current postmaster, is the first woman to hold that position. On paper, that's true. I suspect Lena only served for a few years, then resigned when her growing family began to take up more of her time. A man was chosen for the job, and Lena's efforts were eventually forgotten.

Wondering if that application would have been approved with Lena's name on it? Adam may have done the right thing: The U.S. Postal Service notes that in 1862, only 1.4 percent of the country's 28,586 postmasters were women.

Vigil: 1861

What happened to Helen? If you found the references to her in "Americans," you may have already drawn your conclusions. I'll share my guesses in the notes for that section, in case you haven't read that story yet.

We find out more about Violet's life later in these tales, as well. So, read on!

Welcome, Mr. President: 1876

While this story is completely fictitious, it's true that President Grant traveled a great deal by train.

The Sonberg family has mostly been lost to time, but there is one small bread crumb to be found in the first book of the "Growing Season" series. Melinda Foster, the main character in those books, mentions a set of great-grandparents by the surname of Sonberg who lived near Prosper. I like to think Melinda is a descendant of one of the younger Sonberg boys.

As for the struggles Henry faced, those would be diagnosed as some form of PTSD today. Doctors in the late 1800s had few words for mental-health issues, but the term "soldier's heart" was eventually coined after the Civil War to describe the heart palpitations veterans experienced, along with the fatigue and the emotional challenges that followed them home from the battlefields.

Americans: 1899

Does the last name "Sherwood" ring a bell? The family's furniture store still operates on Eagle River's Main Street more than a hundred years later. Isaac made the changes to the business he talks about here, and also followed through on his vision to create apartments above the store. The sitting room in this story, with its view of Main Street, is the living room in the apartment Kate Duncan rents when she first returns to Eagle River.

Max Sherwood, a recent Eagle River mayor, is Isaac's great-grandson. Max's son, Roland, runs the family business these days and serves as landlord for the tenants living above the store.

As for the Sherwoods' heritage, I suspect those secrets eventually came to light. Isaac didn't seem keen on keeping them, to start with. And if any close relatives took a DNA test, those results would likely reveal hints related to the family's Jewish ancestors.

Moving on to Helen and Pierre: Helen didn't kill him with her knife, as Pierre carried no such wounds when his body was discovered. I'd bet my money on some sort of poison, probably something natural found in the woods, being added to her husband's final bowl of breakfast porridge. I think Helen packed up what was valuable and returned to her native family in the West.

We learn here that Helen's efforts to have a fence placed around the town's burial ground were successful. But something changed as that tale was told and retold over the decades. Sadly, it's not surprising that no one remembers it was a Native American girl who came up with the idea.

One Last Song: 1921

Clara Doyle (or Clara Randolph, or Abigail Doyle, or whatever she's calling herself at any given time) is the second "lost girl" in these tales, along with Helen/Winona. We hear a few rumors about her in "Egg Money," and they're very flattering ones. But given Clara's flair for making things sound better than they are, who knows if those tidbits are even true?

Prohibition was a time when joints like Jake's were common. While the place is long gone, I can tell you that the brick kiln across the road was on the sprawling property where Eagle River's resale business is now located. In Book 3 of the series, Kate and Bev get a good look at the vast collection of housewares and antiques housed in the company's series of buildings.

Because Clara's childhood home was among what are now the old bungalows on the northeast side of town, Alex Walsh's current house is just down the street. And his bar, Paul's Place? That business started out as the little "supper club" (wink wink) referenced in this story.

Oswald Baxter is mentioned in the "Mailbox Mysteries" books, so isn't it fascinating to get a glimpse of him as a young man? I think Clara was spot-on in her assessment of her old school chum: He was never going to change.

Egg Money: 1933

Did all the chatter about chickens give you any clues? The Elmer and Gladys Kleiner farm, with its brick foursquare farmhouse, is now Kate Duncan's acreage one mile east of Eagle River.

The Kleiners were successful in creating their egg business, and they built the grand chicken coop Gladys envisioned sometime during the 1940s. It still stands on Kate's farm, along with the old pump house and a machine shed, but the barn is long gone.

Gladys and Elmer had at least one more child, a daughter, in the very late 1930s. Her name is Minnie. I'm not sure about Louisa, but Minnie did indeed marry "one of those Trowbridge boys from down the road." While Minnie doesn't appear in these tales, we get to meet Will in "Seeds of Discontent."

By the time the "Mailbox Mysteries" series opens, Will has passed away, and Minnie's put the family's acreage on the market because she's moving into town.

On the Shelf: 1945

Irene's dilemma was a common one for women as the soldiers returned home from World War II.

I like to think that when it became more common for married women to teach, Irene went back to the classroom, if even just part time. As we hear in "Seeds of Discontent," Leo did start that seed corn business on the side. I'm sure Irene played an important role there, as well.

Eagle River's Carnegie library is still in use today. Andrew Carnegie, a Scottish-American businessman who was prominent during the Gilded Age, donated money to build more than 2,500 libraries in the late 1800s and early 1900s.

Wikipedia.com notes that the push to build public libraries coincided with the increasing number of women's clubs that were active after the Civil War. Supporting education was a priority for such groups, so I'd bet money on the Eagle River Ladies' Aid Society campaigning to get their town selected as a Carnegie library site.

Speaking of buildings, the post office hasn't changed much since then, either, although Postmaster Schupp would love to cut through all that federal red tape to make some much-needed improvements.

Edmund Freitag, the president of the library board during Irene's tenure, has a descendant who is very active in Eagle River these days. In addition to running the coffee shop, Austin Freitag is the current president of the chamber of commerce.

Tea Party: 1956

Today, Myrtle Bradford is in her nineties and is one of Eagle River's oldest residents. Edwin has since passed away, but she still lives in their grand old house on Oakland Avenue. I suspect she gave up the cigarettes a long time ago, which greatly increased her chances of living as long as she has.

To this day, her house is a favorite stop for Eagle River's mail carriers, even if it's for far-different reasons than why Brock Stevens liked to linger on her porch.

Did she have an affair with Brock? Who knows? Myrtle

has always treated her help incredibly well. If anyone knows the answer to that one, they've never said a word.

The Bradford scholarship fund still hands out grants to Eagle River's graduating seniors.

This story also ties up the loose ends regarding Clem Bradford, Adam Baxter's childhood friend and business associate. He certainly did well for himself!

Seeds of Discontent: 1982

This one hits close to home for our friend Kate Duncan. Lillian and James are her grandparents; Curtis is her father.

This story is rather grim, but there is one positive outcome of note: James and Lillian obviously were able to save their farm, because those acres, and both of the houses, are still in the family.

Kate's brother, Bryan, and his wife now live in the farmhouse inhabited by James and Lillian during this story. After Curtis' grandparents retired and he married Charlotte, they moved into the larger, slightly newer farmhouse just up the road. That home is where Kate and Bryan grew up.

The farm crisis of the 1980s, and its devastating effect on the Midwest, is well documented. Lillian's idea for a mental-health clinic in such a small town would have indeed been revolutionary for the times.

Night Watch: 2009

This one was the catalyst for spelling out all the connections in these stories. As the final tale, there was no easy way to tell all of you what happened next!

Let's start there: Eugene ditched the pills and got clean.

The engineering thing didn't pan out, but Eugene did turn his love of working on cars into a successful career. Today, he's the proud owner of Eugene's Garage, Eagle River's only auto body shop. I'd like to think Eugene hires not only the best mechanics he can find, but that he's eager to provide meaningful employment for those who may have struggled as he once did.

Wade and Colleen eventually moved to Elm Springs, a nearby town, after they retired. Ray Calcott, Eagle River's current police chief, was hired to replace Wade.

Doctor Murray is retired, too, after eventually moving his practice to Charles City; but his wife, Joan, waits tables a few hours a week at Peabody's Restaurant and is a regular attendee of the morning coffee group there. She can often be found sitting across the table from Chris Everton, who still runs the pharmacy.

So ... did Wade ever learn about the drugs Colleen found in their son's room? I don't know for sure, but I suspect the strong will Colleen inherited from Violet helped her convince Eugene to give them up before anyone else was the wiser.

Of course, it's possible Wade had heard rumors about his son's troubles but had yet to share them with his wife. While she was trying to protect Wade, was he doing the same for her? Hmm ...

But that's life in Eagle River. There's always something going on, another mystery that needs to be solved!

* * *

Are you new to Eagle River?
Don't miss out on Kate's adventures!
Sign up at fremontcreekpress.com/connect
to get news about new titles in the series.

Read on for a sneak peek at the first book,
"The Route that Takes You Home."

Sneak peek:
The Route That Takes You Home

Late July
Rockwell Township

The mail stack held just two envelopes for this address today, nothing unusual.

The farm was the same, Kate decided as she slowed for the rusting mailbox at the end of the long driveway.

What she saw in the pasture, however, caught her attention.

There were several cows milling about, but it was the

woman crouched low to the ground that made Kate tap her brakes sooner than usual. In front of the other woman was another animal, down on its side.

When she saw the mail car roll up, the woman ran down to the road. "Hey!" she shouted from across the fence. "You got a minute? I need help."

Kate leaned out the window. "Are you OK?"

"I am. But this cow's about to deliver, and quick." Her polo shirt had some sort of logo on it, but it was too far away to read.

"I just need an extra set of hands. How about yours?"

It had been years since Kate had helped pull a calf. But she could spare ten minutes. If she locked the car, the mail would stay secure.

"I'm so glad you stopped!" The other woman smiled with relief. "I'm Karen Porter. Prosper Veterinary Services."

Kate let out a gasp of surprise. "You're Karen! Bev Stewart told me all about you." Bev, a retired teacher, was one of the part-timers at the Eagle River post office. "I'm Kate Duncan."

The laboring mother let out another moan. "It's OK, honey." Karen tried to soothe her. "I called for backup," she explained to Kate, "but I don't think this girl wants to wait."

"I'm a bit rusty at this." Kate adjusted her straw hat. "My parents farm, but it's been a while since I've been on calf-delivery duty. Do you come here often?"

"Nope." Karen positioned herself behind the cow, and Kate crawled after her. "Maybe once, if at all? I was just driving by today, on my way from another call, when I spotted this girl in distress. I knocked on the door, but no one seems to be home. I couldn't go on by, leave her like this."

Karen pulled out a pair of long rubber gloves. She motioned for Kate to get shoulder-to-shoulder with her. "I'm going in. When it's time, all I need you to do is help pull."

Kate waited, and then she saw the nose. And finally, two little hooves. Karen gave her a nod, and she reached over and held fast. Between the mother's contractions and Karen's efforts, the newborn came at Kate with more speed than she'd expected. She fell back on her heels just as the afterbirth spilled all over her shorts and shirt.

"There we go!" Karen shouted. She gave the calf a quick examination, then nodded. "I think Mama can take it from here." Another truck had just turned up the lane. Karen rolled her eyes and laughed. "There's my assistant, if you can call him that. You're much easier to work with than he is."

An older man carefully stepped down from the cab, then reached back inside for a tackle box.

"Who is that?" Kate raised her eyebrows.

Karen snorted. "Thomas McFadden, doctor of veterinary

medicine." She nodded vigorously as Kate's eyes widened in surprise. "Yeah, he's still licensed. It's a long story, but I'm sure he'd love to tell you every bit of it. Thank goodness you have mail to deliver so you can make your escape."

Karen's business partner, John "Doc" Ogden, was almost back to his usual self after being sidelined for several weeks due to an on-the-job injury. Thomas, Prosper's retired veterinarian, had insisted on helping out until Doc was fully mended. The only problem? His opinions on female veterinarians skewed to the negative.

"Did I miss the party?" Thomas seemed genuinely disappointed when he ambled up to Kate and Karen. "Pulled many a calf in my time. Why, I'll never forget this one, in the summer of 1974, I was ..."

"Thomas," Karen interrupted. "This is Kate Duncan, mail carrier and volunteer vet tech. She beat you to it, I'm afraid."

Kate swallowed her laughter and waved.

"Well, now." Thomas pushed his white hair out of his face. It was surprising how much of it he had left. "You mean to tell me, you girls handled this all on your own?"

Kate pointed at her soiled shirt, which was probably beyond saving. "I believe so."

Thomas scanned the yard as they walked back to their vehicles. "This place feels ... deserted." He pointed to the front of the house. "The grass is dead, like there's usually a vehicle parked by the porch. It rained hard last night, and two nights before that. But there are no ruts in the dirt, nothing at all."

"They must be on vacation, then." Karen dumped her gloves into a plastic tote in her truck's bed. "I'll ask Doc what he wants to do. We can just mail out a bill."

Thomas guffawed. "Milton Benniger, on vacation? He's an old bachelor farmer. Well, I don't know if he's really old." The quick correction told Kate that Milton must be close to Thomas's age. "But anyway, he's not one to jet off to Hawaii. Charles City's about as far as he gets."

Thomas surveyed the yard again. The air shimmered with heat, the oppressive silence broken only by the occasional chirp of a bird. He shook his head, then started for the barn. "I don't like how this feels."

"What are you doing?" Karen marched after him, Kate right behind. "We don't have permission to ..."

"Nonsense! It's just the barn. I don't know what we're looking for, but I'm not ready to leave yet." Thomas slid the door's iron latch to the side, then glanced over his shoulder at the house. "We may go there next. I can't put my finger on it, but something's just not right."

"The Route That Takes You Home"
is available in Kindle, paperback, hardcover
and large-print paperback editions.

The Growing Season books

*Don't miss any of the titles in this heartwarming
rural fiction series*

She's back in her hometown for only a season. But is she secretly searching for a reason to stay?

Melinda is desperately in need of a fresh start when a family dilemma brings her back to her small-town roots. She finds herself behind the counter of her family's store in the charming community of Prosper, and responsible for a rundown farm and a pack of stubborn animals that test her resilience and open her heart.

As she strengthens family ties and forges new friendships, Melinda begins to thrive. But when storm clouds arrive on her horizon, can she hold on to what she's worked so hard to create?

Filled with memorable characters, from a big-hearted farm dog to the weather-obsessed owner of the local co-op, "Growing Season" celebrates the hope and healing found in the small joys of life. Discover this emotional, inspiring series filled with uplifting moments, new beginnings and second chances!

**FOR DETAILS ON ALL THE TITLES
VISIT FREMONTCREEKPRESS.COM**

www.ingramcontent.com/pod-product-compliance
Lightning Source LLC
Chambersburg PA
CBHW021712190726
48289CB00008B/2498